PENGUIN BO

TO BE SACRED

Hyejin Kim has sailed with whales in the Salish Sea, studied hieroglyphs along the Nile, made kimchi in Scandinavia, immersed herself in the underbelly of Northeast China, and run a school in the tropics. Born in South Korea, she teaches and does research at universities in Singapore and Sweden. Her previous books include *Jia: A Novel of North Korea*; a book on Chinese culinary culture, and monographs on business and education. She has best friends and muses in her son and husband.

To Be Sacred

HYEJIN KIM

PENGUIN BOOKS
An imprint of Penguin Random House

PENGUIN BOOKS

Penguin Books is an imprint of the Penguin Random House group of companies
whose addresses can be found at global.penguinrandomhouse.com

Published by Penguin Random House SEA Pte Ltd
40 Penjuru Lane, #03-12, Block 2
Singapore 609216

Penguin Random House SEA

First published in Penguin Books by Penguin Random House SEA 2026

10 9 8 7 6 5 4 3 2 1

ISBN 9789815058796

Typeset in Georgia by MAP Systems, Bengaluru, India

www.penguin.sg

Dedicated with all my heart to the humans who made inyeon with me. Above all, for my best inyeon—Erik and Gustav!

Chapter 1
Lucky Moon

25 December 2015

The sounds didn't stop. Crying, moaning, an intermittent scream . . . Noises of pain reverberated through Park. Day and night. He still wasn't used to it. He had a headache. The noise hit the white walls, bouncing back through his ears and into his head.

'Dr Park, get some sleep. We've had nobody for an hour,' said Nurse Min.

Leaning against the counter, Park must have been frowning again.

'Did Dr Lee come back yet?'

Park tried to smile at Nurse Min. He didn't make eye contact with her. He was sure she hadn't looked him in the face either. It had become a common practice, this casualness. Whether surrounded by screams or silence, they did not have time to greet each other or make eye contact.

Instead of smiling back at him, she turned to the large clock that stood against the wall.

'In ten minutes . . . She said she was swamped with some papers.' Nurse Min tried to defend him, but she was a bad liar. 'She must almost be here.' Her voice sounded less confident.

'Don't worry, I can wait till she comes back.'

Still leaning against the counter, Park swiftly turned away from Min. Without further comment, Min buried her head in some documents on the desk. Everyone knew Dr Lee would be around for just a matter of months, before being transferred up. She was on the fast track. She was the heir to this white castle. Her only obligation now was to kill time here.

Park couldn't leave the emergency room to the interns. It was Christmas night. He knew that an hour of silence meant that the following hours would be hell. The beds were already full. The hospital was far from the city but look at them! All those drunken guys!

Christmas festivities invited fights. It happened every year. Some holiday spirit. People fought and ended up in the hospital. Even when their treatment was done, revellers were slow to leave. They wanted to wait for the police. The police were popular on Christmas. The police had better things to do. It was unlikely they would show up out here. Before the next pack of troubled people came, these people should leave. Their complaints and shouting tormented Park.

Beyond the thick glass door there would be peace and silence. The lucky moon was out. It had been thirty-eight years since the last lucky moon on Christmas. It was a special night. Park had never seen a cold full moon on Christmas. 2015 had been a strange year. Months back, there had been a blood moon. Dripping red, like it was gorging itself on some beast through an invisible mouth. The blood moon prompted stories. 'Something terrible is coming,' people had said. 'The end of this messed up world.' *Why not?* Park thought. There was anticipation of dramatic change, no matter how bad. Fear and excitement had brought sleepless nights.

Nothing had happened. The blood moon had been everything and then was gone. The disappointment was great. No one wanted to talk about it any more.

Tonight was something else. This moon was everything its twin was not. Just as round and full, but calm, piercing the clear sky with confidence. The lucky moon will keep people up. They will be out celebrating Christmas and casting wishes to that glorious orb. Dr Park never celebrated Christmas. Not because he was not religious. It was a Western holiday. *It's not ours*, he thought. No gifts for the kids. His stubbornness upset his wife. 'We could have some fun without overthinking it,' she complained.

Park was stuck in this hell. At night, with the darkness outside and the bright white lights inside, the hospital was a realm apart from its surroundings. Even the moonlight did not enter. The thought of the patients' screams filled him with terror. *Maybe I should go out now and inhale the spirit of the lucky moon*. He thought it might bring some peace to his mind.

Park felt a chill creep over his body. A sharp silence pierced his right ear. Then it dulled and was eventually replaced by a deadly silence. All his senses rushed to his right ear. He turned his head and saw the thick glass of the door slide open. With caution. That's the only way he could describe it. He was used to the door to the emergency ward opening abruptly. Nobody entered timidly. Sometimes, he thought making the door from glass was a mistake—it could break at any moment given the way it was treated. Now, though, the door slid open carefully, deliberately. Even the air seemed to be affected by the gentle touch.

A figure entered. The figure carried silence with him. The silence and peace of the world beyond the glass seeped in. For a moment, Park had a reprieve from the sounds that had tormented him. But somehow this wasn't a comforting quiet. The man approached with a slow, steady stride. Park could hear the slow ticking of the clock. Something was in the man's hand, which he held up in front of him. It was like a sacred gesture. The corridor became a stage for his performance, a temple for his ritual.

Is he bringing the lucky moon? Some holy object was being delivered. The atmosphere changed. Park turned fully towards the newcomer. He squinted. The man wasn't that far away but Park still couldn't see his face clearly. Or maybe it wasn't important.

What sacred thing is he bringing, along with this silence?

Something dripped from the man's elbow, hitting the floor after trickling down his arm. *Drip, drop.*

The dripping reverberated in the silence.

He walked directly towards Park. A supplicant approaching an oracle. The sacred object was coming to him.

From the counter, Park couldn't take his eyes off the stranger's hand. The stranger stopped right in front of him. His action showed he had been targeting Park.

Park saw it. And then he was eye to eye with the stranger.

The stranger held out his hand to Park, displaying the object he was carrying. A white container, round as the lucky moon. *Maybe I was right,* Park briefly thought. With his other hand, the stranger lifted off the face of the moon. He cracked the full moon. The moon opened wide and displayed its mysterious contents. There was something inside. A gooey redness filled the moon.

Park stared in disbelief. *Is it the blood moon? Is he actually delivering the blood moon?* The thing was whole. He could make out all its parts. His face twitched. Identifying the stranger was no longer important.

The stranger finally opened his mouth and said in a husky voice, 'Take it.'

Park looked at the stranger. And before he knew, he himself was holding the blood moon. He drew a blank. No further word from the stranger. No question from Park, either.

The entire scene finally became clear to Park, as details swept over him. The stranger's shirt was covered in blood, which had left a trail down the white hall.

Park looked at the object in his hands. It was a human heart. A pumping heart.

Chapter 2
Fate, Inyeon

September 2010

'Look at him. He's smiling at you again.'

Gun ignored Yoon's comment, but he started walking fast.

'That handsome pervert can't hide his love today.' Yoon chuckled.

Gun glared at Yoon with disdainful eyes. But no response. He didn't want to make any comment. He didn't want any attention at this moment either. He scurried to the main gate of the building. He almost bumped into another boy but managed to jerk himself away fast. He sighed with relief. What he wanted was to be out of the man's view. Putting both hands in the tight pockets of his pants, Gun started to jump up the steps. He went fast but calmly. His body was tense.

The whole situation perplexed him. He could feel his face go red from the tension in his body.

Yoon didn't give up and chased after Gun. 'Hey, why are you so snippy? I'm not teasing. I'm trying to help you!'

Yoon tossed his arm around Gun's shoulder. At least they were out of the man's sight.

Now, Gun opened his mouth and directed his temper at Yoon.

'Why don't you stop it with your ridiculous conclusions?' Gun said with cold eyes.

'I'm just worried about you, friend. Although he's your neighbour, or big daddy, or whatever your parents say, I think he's a fugitive or some paedophile who's done nasty crimes.' For emphasis, Yoon's arm, wrapped around Gun's shoulder, squeezed Gun. Jerking away, Gun walked into the classroom and put his bag down on his desk.

'He has been a good neighbour. What are you saying? Just shut up . . . you are buzzing around like some mosquito in my ear,' said Gun.

Yoon sat next to him, not going to his own desk. Yoon's obsession never stopped. Especially when it had to do with anything about Gun. Gun knew Yoon always acted like he was Gun's closest friend. He was pushing the idea even harder today. *You are the one acting like a stalker*, Gun thought.

'But isn't it weird? You said he's wealthy. Why is he doing this kind of job then? Opening and closing the high school gate every day? And wandering around a stinky boys' school?' Yoon grinned at Gun and came closer.

'Take your stinky mouth away from me first.' Gun pushed Yoon's face away. Yoon's ridiculousness must be the result of his low IQ, or too much time spent staring at his phone. But he didn't stop.

'Or, he has too much money, but nothing to do. He found the perfect target to escape from the boredom of his life.'

Yoon saw the desk's rightful owner walk into the classroom, but he didn't move and continued to occupy the seat next to Gun's and kept jabbering.

'A wealthy man becomes the school gate guy . . . Suspicious . . . It is very fishy . . . and his eyes are always on you, and smiling . . . but very creepy . . . They show that in this universe only Gun exists.' Yoon gesticulated as he spoke, then he sprang up from his chair. He faced the other way and hugged himself, wiggling his arms ridiculously. 'Oh, Gun.' He giggled while he shook his waist right and left erotically. His body bounced back towards Gun. Yoon's smile showed his satisfaction with his own disgusting performance. He sat down in the chair again.

Gun had a strong desire to smack his friend. He stared at Yoon and coldly told him to stop. He yanked Yoon's chair. 'Go back to your own desk!'

Yoon almost tumbled.

'Yo . . . stop it. Okay, I'm leaving.'

Yoon got to his feet and approached Gun again. He whispered, 'We should sneak into his house. We might find some weird things there. Who knows, maybe he has some photos of you taking a shower or something?'

Gun peered at Yoon with anger and pushed him again. 'Go to your seat.'

'Okay, okay . . . but we really should do it. We might be able to discover his secret life. We need to find out about this rich dude. Otherwise, he might eat you up first.'

Before Gun could grab him, Yoon ran to his seat.

What a great start to the day! Gun bit his molars tightly.

★★★

'Now he even shows up at school,' Gun remonstrated to his mother from the edge of the kitchen.

Gun's mom, Young, was focusing on washing the dishes. They had just gotten a dishwasher.

Young sang a song for a dishwasher, and finally, they got one. But she was still washing the dishes by hand. She complained that the steel bowls occupied too much space in the machine. Such a waste of water and electricity. She didn't pay attention to Gun.

'Mom,' he appealed again. Gun felt she'd heard him but was taking the liberty of ignoring him.

When he called for her again, she finally turned off the water. She was met with Gun's brusque face.

'Gun. I heard you. Why do you care about his presence? He's doing his job.'

'It bothers me.'

Young shook her head with a sigh. Gun had always had a temper. He could make a mountain out of a molehill. When something bothered him or he didn't feel comfortable with something, he simply rejected it. Not crying or whining like other kids. He simply and completely walked away from whatever it was or pushed it away. The only son they had didn't like cuddling or warm affection. *That tick was on display again,* Young thought.

Minsu sat down at the kitchen table and chimed in. 'Isn't it better our nice neighbour works there?' Young made eye contact with Minsu. His eyes showed he was on the same page as his wife.

Gun met his father's comment with a dispirited face. 'No. I don't like it. He is always staring at me . . . and giving me a weird smile. Friends talk. I feel stifled when I see him at school.'

Wiping her wet hands on her apron, Young joined them at the table, across from Gun.

'Gun, don't be mean. Your school needs a security guard to take Mr Chang's place during the months he is away. And Jihoon is helping your school.'

Gun's reply was curt. 'It doesn't make sense. Didn't you say he has so much money? Why does he work as a guard at a high school?'

'What kind of logic is that, Gun? He's already retired. He is doing all this for the community! And it is just temporary. He even donated some money to your school.'

Gun stood up and lightly kicked the leg of the chair he had been sitting on.

'I don't like him,' he huffed.

Gun's mom tried to console him.

'Gun, he is a very nice guy. And he is your guardian.'

'I know he is my guardian. I know he promised you guys he would give or lend, or whatever, some money. It's pathetic.' Young's eyes were wide with surprise as she stared at Gun. Minsu grabbed Young's hand.

Gun blushed and his frustration showed.

'I just don't like him. He sometimes looks at me through the window of the classroom with that weird fucking smile. His face shows I'm his money slave,' he said, flushed with anger.

Gun's father and mother looked at each other in surprise but tried not to show their shock to Gun.

'My friends make fun of me. They find it hilarious that I am that pervert's true love.'

'Gun, watch your mouth,' Minsu frowned.

Gun was raving and kicked the chair again, harder this time.

'I'm stressed out because of him, Dad. This is excessive stress that I can't bear. I don't even want to go to the toilet alone at school. I have to focus on my classes for the exam. There are only a few months left till the university exam. When I see that guy, I want to punch him in the face. If I fail the exam or if I am dragged away by the police, it will be all your fault. I don't want his money. I don't want him to be near me.'

Gun stormed to his room.

Minsu and Young were shocked by their son's anger. Gun didn't usually express his emotions or temper like this. Sometimes, it scared Young. This time was not the usual reaction from Gun.

'What's going on?' She looked at Minsu with a perplexed face. 'Shall we tell him?'

'No, we all agreed not to say anything,' replied Minsu.

'But look at our son. He had a meltdown. We don't want him to be distracted from his studies now. We have to tell Jihoon. This is not good . . .'

'I will sort it out,' Minsu said with a furrowed brow.

'Honey, we didn't want money from Jihoon. We can afford things by ourselves.'

'But we don't need to refuse either.'

Minsu tried to appease Young. She was unnerved by her husband's preoccupation with Jihoon's money.

'I will sort it out. Let's calm down. Gun is just sensitive now and nervous because of the exam.' Minsu stood up awkwardly from the chair and checked the chair Gun had kicked. It was fine, of course, but Minsu wanted to escape Young's gaze.

'He is already a teenager full of secrets. I don't want him to be more distant,' said Young.

'Okay, okay. Just remember that Gun is at the most sensitive age. He will get over it. He was fine with Jihoon before. I will talk to Jihoon first, and then Gun. Everything will be all right.'

Young stood up from the chair with a sigh. She turned the water on. She somehow felt useless. That feeling touched a nerve. She started washing dishes again, with noisy clanks—the steel bowls were perfect for these moments. Her anger and frustration were channelled into the dishes. It had been a good decision to go for stainless steel.

Minsu stared at Gun's firmly closed door. He thought that he would call Jihoon tomorrow.

When Minsu had heard about Jihoon's nice gesture to temporarily serve as the security guard for the school, he had grunted. *What is this rich guy doing? Isn't Jihoon's excessive generosity receiving enough praise in this neighbourhood? At this rate, he would be a local politician next.* Minsu was uncomfortable. But he knew that Jihoon presented opportunities for him. That was hard to resist.

★★★

Young opened the front door. It was Jihoon. He stood there, a charming smile on his face, wearing a white shirt and blue jeans. Before Young could do anything, Jihoon said, 'I brought some lettuce and sesame leaves. Fresh ones . . . just from my garden.' Jihoon lifted a basket and waved it in front of Young's eyes. The lettuce and sesame leaves were well organized, and they looked fresh. The fragrance of the sesame leaves was overwhelming. It drew her in. Even the oversized straw basket looked fancy. *Maybe it is a high-end basket*, Young thought.

'These will go well with *gogi*. I ordered some *hanu*. It was just slaughtered in Yecheon. It will be delivered to your house this afternoon.'

The basket was in Young's hands.

'You didn't have to, Jihoon.'

'Perfect combination of protein and vitamins! Enjoy it with your family.' Jihoon offered a smile.

Gun is a bastard, even though he is my son.

Young felt sad each time she saw Jihoon's smile. How could Gun treat the man as a monster? Jihoon hadn't changed much in ten years. He was still good looking. And he didn't look fifty. His silver hair only made people wonder about his real age. Against Jihoon's youthful face, his hair seemed to have absorbed all of his ageing.

Thanks to Jihoon's organic garden, he was naturally tanned. It was not a gardener's tan, but it looked like a tan from the beach. His garden was popular among the neighbourhood ladies. Of course, his status as a wealthy, available man in early retirement made the men jealous. But the husbands eventually took a shine to Jihoon. He did not go around bragging. In fact, he never talked about himself. He had a habit of making light conversation—light but engaging. His generosity in sharing vegetables and his willingness to help won him the community's admiration.

Gun doesn't know how lucky he is.

Jihoon seemed to hurry away, then casually noted, 'Oh, by the way, I quit my job at the school.'

Young suddenly felt herself blush. She lowered the vegetable basket, which suddenly felt heavy. 'Oh . . . did you . . .'

'I talked with Minsu. I was inconsiderate. I was just happy to see Gun at school. Maybe I smiled at him too much when I saw him . . . you know. It wasn't intentional. Maybe just my brain responding to my neighbour. I didn't know that it had made him uncomfortable.'

Young came out of the doorway. She was embarrassed. 'Oh, Jihoon. I am so sorry . . . this child is getting more difficult.' Young was shocked that Minsu had shared Gun's reaction with Jihoon already. Did he really have the guts to do that? Or were they these close friends now? Neither seemed right.

'Young, of course we should understand. It's not an easy time. He wants to go to university. It's competitive and his mind is on exams. I hadn't seen it from his viewpoint. That's absolutely my fault . . .'

'I am sorry, Jihoon. I did yell at him. His attitude keeps getting worse.'

Jihoon tossed another attractive smile at Young.

'Set your mind at rest, Young. Really, maybe my thinking was too simple. When the school needed a temporary security guard, I just thought, why not? While the regular fellow is off seeing his daughter and newborn grandson, I thought I could help a little at the school. The principal is a good friend of mine, you know. And I have never had such a job . . . so I thought it could be fun.' Jihoon shrugged slightly. He seemed to be working to persuade Young that the episode was not a big deal for him. That embarrassed Young more.

'You didn't have to quit . . . Everyone knows your intention except this unbelievably annoying kid.'

'No, no. I just can't hide my happiness when I see Gun. But yes . . . Gun is a teenager and now he is preparing for his exams. I should have been more sensitive. He and I will be fine again soon. I don't want to be hated by him either. That . . . hurts more than anything else.'

Young saw Jihoon's pain.

'Jihoon, I will remind him. Gun does not hate you. He is negative about everyone these days.'

Jihoon grinned. 'I know. Weren't we all like that once? Hating everyone and the world when we were teenagers? Enjoy your dinner with *hanu* and greens.'

'Jihoon, do you want to join us?' Young wanted to make up for this awkward moment.

'Thanks . . . but I have a dinner appointment with friends. Enjoy!'

Jihoon walked away.

How can anyone think he is weird?

Young watched Jihoon enter his own home, looking back so they could wave to each other. Then Young went in and closed the door behind her.

She thought that she would talk with Gun once more.

Chapter 3
Lucky Moon and Rebirth

25 December 2015

Jihoon had targeted the hospital long ago. Someone he could trust should fix this problem again. Luckily, they were all there. Jihoon knew Dr Lee had moved there. Her junior, Dr Park would be working. Jihoon searched for a new body. There was a perfect new body with Dr Lee. A healthy twenty-six-year-old woman.

Mr See could have found a better one in the beginning. That had been such a failure. He shouldn't have been chosen at all.

The full moon guided Jihoon on his path. It seemed to assist his mission. The hospital was surrounded by pine trees. They must have been protected for centuries. Even the Japanese hadn't destroyed this forest. Maybe because there had been no tigers here, or if they were, they must have at least been fewer than around the other mountains. There were no mines or rice farms nearby. Not worth exploiting this place. The trees could survive.

A broad mountain embraced the building. Her wide arms provided protection from the sides while her peak looked out over the top and into the distance.

She is like a mother, giving unconditional love to this solitary hospital, Jihoon had thought.

It must be tonight.

The forest helped him perfectly complete his mission. The sky studded with stars. Such a beautiful night! He had been able to hide the RV in the bushes on a side road two days ago. No one had seen him move the vehicle. He needed to finish everything within an hour. The body was still. Jihoon was strong; he worked out regularly and followed a strict diet. It was not an easy job to do on one's own. He couldn't have done it without her. At least, the first mission had been accomplished successfully. She had done a great job. It was his turn to take over and to finalize the mission. He focused. He went through the order a hundred times in his mind. There shouldn't be any mistake. He shouldn't skip anything.

He thought he would be sad. He was not. He impressed himself. There was no remorse. Even the anger had disappeared. The trees around him absorbed his emotions—the fear, the rage, the sadness. Jihoon had been nervous in the beginning, but while he was opening the chest, a flutter of excitement passed through him. He was thrilled at the prospect of seeing her again soon! *Let's focus on her.*

Although it was Jihoon's first time, he had done surprisingly well. He was unfazed. When the breastbone was opened, there she was. Alive. His eyes were full of tears. He closed them for a moment. *Calm, calm. I do everything with thought, accurately and swiftly. The clock is ticking . . . there is no time for this.* He was ready to carry out the cardioplegia. He would wait till she fell asleep. Jihoon delivered a jolt of electricity, immediately causing the pumping action to slow. 'Wait, my girl. I will make you lively again soon,' he murmured to himself.

He tried not to forget what he had imagined doing so many times. All that practice. The blood vessels should be managed carefully. *Pulmonary artery, inferior vena cava, superior vena cava, atrium . . .* The lucky moon made his work sacred. 'It is,' he whispered, 'it is a sacred job.' His knees flexed when he took her out from the body. Joy surged through him at that moment.

I'm sorry, my sweet. How stupid I was! How much did you suffer here?

Carefully, Jihoon put her in a round container he had prepared. She floated in the cold saline solution. That container fitted into a larger one of the same shape. An icy fog oozed out of the inner layer. He had searched long to prepare the container, specially designed for this purpose. He had gone three times to Singapore, five times to Dubai. All the work to find the medical centres there that were willing to show him how it was done, and then the observing and the practice.

He held the container gingerly. It felt as big as the full moon behind him. Holding it reverently, he stood up. His job was done. Without even a glimpse at his girl's keeper of several years, he turned away and opened the door of the RV. A cold wind from the dark hit his face. *Welcome to the new world*. He smiled. Carefully stepping down, he walked towards the hospital. The moon followed him, showing the way. Was the moon confused that it might be her lost baby?

She will be born again.

He entered the hospital. He entered the loving embrace of mountain mama.

Chapter 4
Hana

27 December 2015

'Another psycho? Come on . . . this is not fair. Why me, again?' Hana was already driving to Kangwon, talking on her mobile phone with her manager.

'Sir, will you take responsibility if I go crazy because of the stress?' she continued.

Hana opened the driver's side window. The mountains enticed her to taste the fresh wind. It was cold. The mountains were full of snow. She opened the passenger side window as well. She shivered. Cold, but fresh. She had hiked Mt. Sullak when she was in a hiking club in her university days.

That was the best time of my life.

Since then, her hectic life meant being stuck in the city's concrete. Of course, the misery of polluted surroundings was the bonus.

She knew that it had all been planned. *Passing all these psychopaths off to me. That way they can put a lid on me. You will see who will be knocked down first.* She sighed and put the windows back up.

'Don't you understand them better than anyone else here?'

The voice over the phone brought her back to reality. Her fleeting pleasure from the cold wind was immediately gone.

'What do you mean?' She frowned.

'Isn't your nickname "psycho"?' The voice on the other end snorted. 'My gosh . . . That's a pretty name!'

When Hana heard that, she was momentarily speechless and disconcerted. Hana had earned the nickname 'psycho' when she had confronted her superior, Nam. It had a been two years earlier. She had been labelled a psycho, and she had also learnt that Nam was a great actor.

The day she'd got her nickname; she had been summoned by Nam. He had intentionally called Hana into a meeting room that had a big window through which everyone could see them. She had just questioned him because she really thought he had taken dirty money from Sammi, one of the biggest conglomerates.

'How close are you with them?'

Hana had put the question to Nam. She was glad he'd faced her directly. She'd done the same as well. Hana had told Nam that she had suspected him because an anonymous whistle-blower had submitted a report.

If the whistle-blower was right, and if Nam was the deliveryman taking money to prosecutors and judges for Sammi, her company would be in trouble. But nobody wanted to investigate. They were afraid of Nam or Sammi. Is that just how it goes? What about the media? If the whistle-blower went to the media, what would they do? Or maybe everyone except her was in league with Nam. Perhaps the whistle-blower was one of her colleagues who hoped Hana would do the tough part.

Nam was a performer. In the mornings, he walked in singing opera. *I'm an elegant fellow!* His face beamed with pride when he walked in, singing and with a colourful scarf around his neck. His thick, black-rimmed spectacles showed his pretention. *I'm an intellectual!* The not-so-hidden lift in the soles of his shoes indicated that he wanted to be bigger than he was.

Still, Hana had not expected Nam's drama would go that far. After she had told him about her suspicions, Nam had thrown a drinking glass in her direction. The crash when it had hit the floor had made everybody look their way.

The room was a stage. She immediately understood why he had chosen that office. Everyone's eyes were on them.

Puffing himself up, Nam screamed, 'You psycho!' He trembled, and his face flushed. Everyone knew he was infuriated. Everyone knew they were not supposed to ask their manager uncomfortable questions. Everyone knew how to tread lightly around Nam. Nobody touched him. Shrinking one's ego was the first lesson in the office. That had been accepted by everyone. Except Hana.

That's how Hana had become the psycho. Her bold move was interpreted as impertinence among colleagues. Or they were jealous. She had done what others couldn't do.

Nam clearly wanted to warn other people not to question him. But the real reason why everyone called Hana psycho was because of the way Hana had looked at Nam at that moment. Pieces of glass had been scattered everywhere, but Hana had still peered straight at Nam in wonder . . . no fear and no anger. Her eyes had still sought an answer from Nam. Those inquisitive eyes made others believe that she was the true psycho. Hana asked Nam one more time, 'So did you really get money from Sammi?' Her eyes had been telling him that she wanted to get to the bottom of the matter.

Since that time, things had changed. Nam had never acknowledged the accusations to be true, but everyone knew that he had taken big money from Sammi. He left the company. So, Hana had been right. His reason for resigning was unambiguous. 'I can't work with a crazy stalker in the office!'

Nam still worked as an expensive lawyer in his own firm. His company directly worked for Sammi, especially on the most unpleasant matters. Instead of directly joining the company's legal department, he had his own firm and claimed that he was open for doing business with anyone, rich or poor. One by one, smart and ambitious colleagues disappeared. Their faces popped up in Nam's company. Hana's law firm started losing their clients.

Hana had done the right thing, but she couldn't be invited into their club. Nobody wanted to be around her. She felt she owed her company, that it was her fault they were losing many old clients to Nam's new firm. Although Hana was right, her nickname didn't go away. The difficult cases, and the ones with the strangest criminals, landed on her desk.

'I just got done with the psycho from Daegu,' she complained to herself. *Another rich psycho? How much money did this monster throw at our company? We will be known for defending all these crazy, dangerous men who think they can get away with anything because of their money or power.*

She had just completed the case of a thirty-year-old man who had killed his parents and his older sister—stabbed them dozens of times each—then gone to play computer games in a PC room, where the police arrested him.

'I stabbed each exactly thirty times—once for each of the pain they gave me,' the man had proudly told Hana. He stretched his arms to the left and right side in front of Hana. *Is he trying to show how hard he'd worked?* Hana watched his indulgent gesticulation.

'It was my birthday,' he continued. Defending that one was difficult. Hana grumbled to herself.

A criminal psychologist had told her before, 'Many criminals tend to focus on extrinsic elements. So, the fault lies with the people or environment around them.' The psychologist continued, 'But revolutionaries or people who change the world have a similar tendency. They make revolutions in order to change what is around them.' This had been the response when Hana had asked the psychologist whether such people were worth defending.

Was it his revolution?

What she learned from the murderer was that he had always been compared to his sister, who seemed smart and went to a top university and found work in a big company. She was about to marry. But she was embarrassed about her younger brother, who was the troublemaker in the family, had gone to a mediocre university, and hadn't been able to find a job for several years. She hadn't taken him to the two-family meeting, when she and her future-husband had introduced their families to each other. That must have provoked him. His anger had prompted him to invent his own version of the family story. He was not smart enough because his mom didn't eat good food when she was pregnant with him. His dad was absent his whole childhood because of his own busy life. He complained about his deceased parents to Hana.

'Nothing I did was wrong. They didn't want me. They wanted to get rid of me. There was no choice for me. It's like a survival game. Before they killed me, I had to find a way to survive.'

Hana was scared. She was scared for herself, not because of him, but because she was listening to his story. At first, she thought she needed to listen to him because he was her client. Later, she found herself considering what a difficult position he had been in. Society is full of crazy competition. People are easily jealous of others. We compare. We are compared. The family should protect each other and understand each other.

Wait a minute!

Listen to them, but don't put my emotion in there. Your job is to defend them as a lawyer. I'm walking myself into a dangerous zone.

She was startled. When he noticed that this lawyer was listening to him, he started bragging about the different parts of the body he had targeted on his family members.

She went back to the hotel room and stared at the victims' photos before and after the brutal murder.

The parents had left behind a significant amount of money. Their elderly life could have been pleasant. They had just retired and started getting a decent pension. She found their plans for a cruise to Europe. What was the use of it? Their murderer would be the inheritor of the assets. Following the murderer's line, he was the actual victim of cold parents and sister. His mental status had been on the verge of being destroyed.

Hana was eventually exhausted by her client's persistence that he had been harassed. She had to listen. And that line formed the basis of her defence. His mental sickness, caused by his parents' and sister's harassment, led to this brutal murder.

She couldn't work hard. She felt that she was wasting her time and her life.

And then . . . after the trauma of that case, she had received the call for another murder case. This one was exactly the opposite, it seemed. The perpetrator didn't want to defend himself. He'd actually walked in after he had committed the crime.

On the way, she stopped at a rest area. Her excuse was to eat some food. While eating spicy beef soup, she opened her email.

Maybe I'm attracted to psychos. Maybe I belong to their club.

He'd taken a heart from a person. He had committed the crime right in front of a hospital. A video file from the hospital camera was included. He'd literally taken a beating heart from a young man. The camera showed him delivering a bloody heart to a doctor! The gesture was calm, serene, even sacred. You could see the doctor was standing still. He was part of the audience for the sacred walker. He appeared mesmerized when the murderer presented the moon-shaped container. To Hana, it looked like the doctor had even started to kneel as he'd received the object.

What was going on here?

Was the doctor an accomplice?

She hurriedly finished the soup and started driving. She didn't need the chilly wind any more.

Her heart was thumping.

★★★

Hana walked into the room. He was sitting, still. His clothes were bloody. The blood stains stood out on the white turtleneck sweater. He looked drained, but his face also reflected peace.

'Hi, I'm Hana, your lawyer.'

Hana sat in front of him. He had refused a lawyer. Hana felt she should make sure he knew who she was.

Jihoon lifted his head and looked up, making eye contact with Hana.

'I don't need a lawyer. I'm the one who did it. I should be punished accordingly.'

No fear, no anger. He'd torn apart a living human body and whipped out a still-pumping heart from a healthy, young man. He had left the boy's body in a vehicle in the forest. It had obviously been planned for a long time. The RV had been fitted out specifically for this crime. Medical equipment had been installed.

Hana had expected to meet somebody with frantic eyes.

What is this guy's story? He must have an accomplice. It was hard to believe he had done everything on his own.

But she was confused. If there were a row of potential criminals in front of her, he would be the first person ruled out. Now Hana understood why

Detective Kang had said what he did before she had entered the room.

'He admitted to what he did. And we have clear evidence on the hospital CCTV.' Hana nodded since she had also seen the video clip. Behind her, Kang continued, 'He doesn't say much. Has refused food . . . But in my twenty years on the force, I don't know . . . he is the first of these types that have I felt sympathy for . . . a strange feeling.'

Kang walked down the corridor with Hana. He was still chewing hard. His persistence to stop smoking could pay off this time. He no longer smelled of smoke. Mint instead. Chewing gum, his hair in a buzz cut, Kang looked tough.

'Kang, it's not like you.' Hana looked at Kang with surprise. 'Don't forget that this man slaughtered a human. I heard that he was even not dead at the time.'

'The victim?' Kang smirked. 'Yes . . . the victim . . . we finally found him.'

Hana stopped and looked at Kang, who then also stopped. 'What do you mean? Were you looking for the victim?' Kang's lack of sympathy for the victim was bizarre. It was really not like Kang. He looked like a middle-aged man one could come across anywhere, but he was a great interrogator. When he started an inquisition, his talents shone through. He was the most observant detective Hana had ever met. That's why Hana liked Kang and trusted him.

'I have to thank you, Detective Kang. You make my job easier. You just acknowledged the murderer is not a bad guy . . . and indicated that the victim is rather fishy. Am I right?'

Kang shook his head. 'We will talk about it later. Check the murderer first . . . or saviour, in my book.'

Hana looked at him strangely.

'I owe him in a way. He solved a case that has been giving me such a headache,' Kang sighed and started walking again. Hana followed him.

Kang had a hot-temper, and he was rugged and straightforward. He had no sympathy for criminals. But too many tears for the victims . . . or excuses for him to drink. His reaction to Jihoon and the victim intrigued Hana. There was something more about this case.

'You've got the wrong career. You are more suited to be a prosecutor, not a lawyer,' Kang would tell Hana. Hana sometimes also thought she and Kang could have been a great team if she were a prosecutor.

Hana smiled and said, 'You should share all you have with me this time.'

'You know you work for the criminal. I'm working for the victim,' Kang laughed.

'This time seems a little bit different. Am I right?' Hana responded to him. Her voice couldn't hide her excitement. They reached the room at the end of the corridor and halted in front of the familiar door. Hana knew that, on the other side of the door, she would meet a man who was either another psycho or someone intriguing.

Reading the anticipation on Hana's face, Kang opened the door and said, 'You will have several hours before the team from the prosecutor's office comes. He didn't want a lawyer. I'm letting you in because it is you.' Kang hated Hana's law firm . . . he hated all lawyers from the law firm, except the psycho, Hana. She gestured thanks in his direction.

Walking in the room and looking at the man, Hana understood what Kang had been talking about. Lowering her eyes, she focused on the documents that she had brought.

'I know you don't want a lawyer.'

'I'm a sinner. I'll be punished accordingly.' Jihoon's voice was leaden. Then he added, 'I should be condemned.'

Hana didn't respond to him. What she knew was that his ex-wife had hired her firm to defend the monster sitting in front of her. She wondered why his ex would work so hard to protect him. What kind of life had he lived to end up committing such a horrendous crime and have a former wife who sought to give him costly legal help?

The records showed that he had called his ex after committing the crime. The cameras had caught him on the phone with someone when he'd been waiting for the police to arrive at the hospital. His face had clearly been visible. Hana remembered the expression he'd worn. It was calm and strangely peaceful.

Hana knew that the documents and video didn't mean she understood him. She needed more.

She closed the documents and put them aside, pushing them to the corner of the desk. She took off her coat and hung it on the back of her chair.

'That's not enough. I won't walk away just because you admitted to your crime. Either I dig till I'm satisfied, or you share your story with me. Then, only then, would I consider giving up.'

Jihoon stared at Hana. She looked young. Curiosity in her eyes. No fear . . . so much energy . . . but unflappable round eyes! She must be Mini's age. It made him smile.

Sharing my story with this stranger. Is it the last thing I can do?

The silence between them continued, but they were watching each other. Hana prompted, 'Citron tea? We might be here for some time.'

Jihoon didn't respond, but he didn't say no either.

Hana smiled.

Chapter 5
Ocean Blue

October 2000–May 2001

'It's safe for children.'

The saleswoman's make-up was excessive. It made her stand out from the other saleswomen in the department store.

'What do you mean?' Eunwoo's mom, Nari, couldn't understand at first. *Are others not safe for children?*

'This doesn't use any harmful chemicals.' The saleswoman patted the product as though it were a pet. Her movements were awkward. She was a tall woman. She bent all the way down until her face was nearly up against the item. *Is she some B-grade actress? This must be her side job.* Nearly rubbing her face on the machine, the clerk smiled hopefully up at Nari. *She is posing for a photo.* Nari suppressed a chuckle.

Nari rephrased what the saleswoman had said, 'Are you saying other humidifiers use harmful chemicals?' Nari frowned. 'That's immoral.'

'I know . . . but the companies don't mind as long as they can sell their products.' The saleswoman's voice grew, and she began to gesticulate vigorously. Nari was glad that there were not many people around during this sales period. Otherwise, her strange behaviour would have attracted attention. Right now, however, the few busy shoppers that were there, passed by, giving no notice.

'Our Ocean Blue is different. Look at how clean and fresh-looking she is!' She softly stroked the blue globe. 'And the best news for you is we're issuing a promotional discount on this new model.'

Nari was tempted. The water undulated, waves splashing rhythmically against the glass. The machine whirred pleasantly. She recalled the family vacation to the coast two years ago. That was the most recent family vacation. The clerk's staccato voice pulled her back from that good memory.

'See! This model even has two spouts. Look at them. See how strong they are. With one machine, you can cover the whole house. You don't need separate ones in each room.'

Mist rose out of the spouts. It was more of an aquarium than a humidifier. Nari's thoughts shifted from the beach to the little toy fish Eunwoo liked to play with. She peered at one of the spouts. The mist caressed her face. A strong aroma. Clean, like a hospital, in the best possible way. 'It does smell clean.'

'Of course! It looks great and makes the house smell great.' The saleswoman bent down and inhaled the mist from the other spout. Nari suddenly felt self-conscious. The two women bent over the machine attracted the attention of nearby shoppers. A few gathered around them.

The saleswoman became excited in front of the small crowd. She redoubled her efforts to persuade Nari. 'Nowadays, every house has a humidifier.' She seemed to be shaming her in front of this group. *Why don't you have one yet?* Nari again felt annoyed with the saleswoman and her ridiculous make-up.

Although the saleswoman had not asked Nari directly, she felt she should defend herself from the strangers' eyes surrounding them.

'Ours is too old. We bought it so long ago. We want to purchase a better one this time.' The lie came out unconsciously. Her cheeks became flushed. She knew her voice protested against the saleswoman's public accusation.

'Oh great! Then I strongly recommend this one. You will see a big difference.' The lady's voice rose. 'It's good for your skin too. Your skin will look younger.'

Her gestures grew. Her voice lifted up to soprano.

'You look about thirty now. But if you use this . . .'

Her compliment to Nari was followed with a finale with a big smile. She probably didn't know that her front teeth had her red lip gloss on it.

'If you use this, people will think you're a university student.' Again, the clerk moved her face into the mist, as she beamed at Nari. Maybe she was not a B-grade actress. Maybe she was a master seller.

Nari caved, hating herself for giving in. She had to choose the instalment payment option, spreading the cost over two years.

'It is expensive compared to similar products. But it is worth it.' The saleswoman pointed at the label. 'See, this indicates it's eco-friendly.'

It was twice as expensive as the other brands. *Why am I paying through the nose?* She considered the four members of her family, including herself, and divided the price by four. Thinking about four people feeling pleasant . . . It might be worth it. Winter was coming. She didn't want the whole family to suffer from dryness over the nights the way they had last year. The saleswoman said that by purchasing it now, before winter, she would receive a free pack of disinfectant for the humidifier.

'A twenty-four-bottle box of disinfectant will be delivered to your address together with the humidifier,' she explained as she handed the receipt to Nari.

'You mean for cleaning the machine?' Nari was confused.

The saleswoman looked uncertain for the first time. She picked up a bottle from under the table. She squinted at the fine print. She didn't look old enough to be far-sighted. 'Like I said, it's disinfectant.' It sounded like she was trying to convey confidence.

'So how often do we use it? When we clean the machine?' Nari hurriedly stuffed the receipt in her handbag.

'No, it says . . . you add this . . . to the water. And it says it is disinfectant.'

'So, it is not a cleaner.' Nari wanted to make sure. *At this price, you at least need to provide detailed and accurate information.* She felt her stomach turn, thinking about the price. They were a little bit pinched these days.

The saleswoman again studied the back of the bottle and did her best to make out the letters.

'It's disinfectant. It helps the machine stay clean and the water to remain disinfected. Just add it when you change the water.'

The saleswoman's finger jabbed at the writing. Her long finger nail, half pink and half yellow, covered the text. 'See here. How convenient this machine is. It gets rid of bacteria. If you use this one, it will make your cleaning job much easier. Some brands don't care about hygiene. The humidity attracts bacteria, but this disinfectant will wipe them out.'

Her confidence fully returned as she delivered this lecture. Perhaps her eyes had gotten used to the tiny writing. 'Just follow the instructions and your family will get the most out of it.' She hurried back to her place. Her show, supported by Nari, had been successful. Many people stood in line to check the blue water.

Nari decided not to stop at the other stores on her list. A parka for her husband, Hyuk, could wait till next winter. He still had a good winter coat. Or she could check the second-hand shops next weekend. She felt that if you looked at the big picture, the money wasn't wasted. And the saleswoman was right. Nowadays, every household had a humidifier. In addition, the design oozed quality. And it wasn't the monstrosity that some of these machines could be. There was no horrible sound when it was activated. It would brighten the house. Nobody in the family would suffer waking up with a dry nose. It wouldn't feel like living in the middle of a cold desert. *Not any more.* She grinned as she hurried back to the house. She had to reach home before the deliveryman arrived. She had a spring in her step.

★★★

Dr Moon felt odd.

'There are no available beds,' administrator Park said. He delivered the message with a bit too much perkiness. His face looked happy. *Maybe it's good for the hospital.* Park's beaming face annoyed Moon. Especially today. Too many kids with similar symptoms. And too suddenly. It was now a full two weeks that he had been seeing patients with similar problems daily. Till a couple of weeks ago, he'd only seen it a handful of times in his career.

Moon walked back to his office and sat down in his leather chair with a thud. He fished it out of his pocket. He called his friend Kim.

'Hey, how have you been?' Moon sprang up from his chair and began pacing around the office.

'Busy, busy.' A tired voice came through the phone. 'Did the sun rise in the west today? You're calling me?' Kim's voice was tired, but he seemed happy to get an unexpected call from his old college friend and former colleague.

Moon grinned. 'Does that mean your pockets are getting thicker?'

'Maybe . . . but this sort of business is not welcome,' Kim said over the line.

'What do you mean?' Moon asked with interest.

Moon knew that Kim was swimming in debt, if not drowning. Their friends had said he was crazy to open his own practice so soon. It was too early to be independent. But Kim couldn't stand the hierarchy at the university hospital. He loved hiking and biking. But they all knew they won't have such romantic life for a while, at least not till they finished their medical school. 'Debt from the book or pressure from superiors—which one would kill me first?' Kim chose to walk out of the university hospital. Nobody did that. Their friends thought he had lost it; on some level, they were jealous of his courage. They were jealous of his guts. He opened a small paediatric clinic in the district he'd spent his childhood in. Getting the bank loan wasn't hard, paying it back was the devious part.

Since setting up his clinic, Moon and the other paediatricians rarely saw Kim. He even skipped their monthly gatherings. No time for booze. No time for bonding with his friends. Instead, he stayed open Saturdays to take on more patients.

So, Kim's statement surprised Moon. He should have been delighted to be busy with patients. The more the patients the faster he could repay his bank loan.

Kim sighed. 'You know . . . it's just weird. Nowadays, kids are showing up with the same symptoms. I've already sent two over to a big hospital today.'

'What symptoms?' Moon's voice became tense.

'Breathing with difficulty,' Kim answered monotonously.

Paediatrician Moon gripped his phone tightly. 'Explain.'

'Why are you so interested in my patients? Have you become some sort of medical spy?' Kim chuckled. His voice was still tired, but there was a bit more energy there.

Moon didn't laugh. The speed of his pacing in the small office increased. 'No . . . I've actually noticed a troubling trend as well.'

The voice on the other end finally sounded interested. 'What trend?'

A pause. Then, at the same time, they said, 'Pulmonary fibrosis.'

Silence followed. Moon bit his lower lip. He opened his mouth first. 'Our beds are full of kids with lung injuries.'

'When did it start?'

'Two to three months ago.' Moon stopped pacing and leaned against the office door. Summer was on the way. It was a good time of the year. But the heat of summer had not arrived. May brought a cool breeze and blossoming flowers. That also meant kids coming in with lung issues. But this year was different. This wasn't hay fever. And Moon didn't believe that toddlers would suddenly be exposed to much more severe levels of second-hand smoke. This was not natural. Kids with pulmonary fibrosis. It was usually a disease of smokers or the elderly. What was happening was not something he had anticipated as a paediatrician.

'Are your cases serious?' Moon asked Kim carefully.

'Some are. It's not pneumonia. These kids have severe pneumonia-like symptoms, minus the fever. Why are we dealing with this shit? It should be the geriatrics guys who get this,' returned Kim.

'Acute interstitial pneumonia. That's what I'm saying,' said Moon with a slight change of voice. 'Have you come up with something else?'

'That's my best guess as well,' returned Kim. 'A big part of the lungs has already stiffened. I had two who were in the worst condition. They even developed idiopathic acute respiratory distress syndrome. What could I do in my clinic? So, I immediately sent them to a university hospital.'

Moon's suspicions were confirmed. Maybe Kim made a rash career decision, but he was a cool-headed physician. He wouldn't exaggerate.

After hanging up, Moon returned to his desk. He started typing with purpose. He drafted the email in one go. He knew what to say. He had not written this kind of message before, but he knew he should now. This one would go to a bunch of paediatricians. He might need to contact the Ministry of Health. Something was happening.

★★★

The entire family arrived at the hospital. They had all fallen sick the same day. Hyuk had felt that something was wrong. The dry cough that each of them had had turned severe. He recognized it at dinner. Everyone coughed ceaselessly. Including him. But Hyuk's was the mildest. He realized that the cough they all had wasn't normal. They were coughing longer and more frequently.

'Are you fine? Is it too dry?' Hyuk had asked at dinner.

Nari shook her head. 'No . . . it's not possible.' She glimpsed at Ocean Blue placed prominently next to the sofa. 'Maybe we caught a spring cold. We will be fine.'

Hyuk gave the machine a long look. Its perpetual whirring had become the sound of home. He didn't like Ocean Blue. It had become the family pet. The smell put him off too. *Who wants to be reminded of a hospital at home?* It wasn't fragrant and it covered up the smell of home.

'Do we need that on? It's almost summer.'

Nari shrugged. 'Maybe now . . . it's probably unnecessary now. The kids like Ocean Blue though.'

Hyuk looked at their son Eunwoo and Lia, their daughter. 'We are heading to the real ocean with a real ocean smell soon.' His voice was determined.

I wish I were more present. Hyuk had started coming back home more often than before. He had told his boss that he would work late every other day. The other days he would leave early and catch the 4 p.m. train home. Then, at least, he would be able to sleep at home on alternate nights. After his research centre had moved out of Seoul, the centre had provided a dormitory room for each staff member. Finally, they had decided to move down altogether after this summer. Nari wasn't keen on leaving Seoul.

'It's not easy to leave the place where I was born and grew up,' she had complained. She had imagined that their kids would grow up and go to school in Seoul. Leaving the capital would feel like a downgrade. Although the new town had everything Seoul had, Hyuk understood her disappointment. His colleagues all returned to bachelorhood during the week, then spent the weekend with their spouses or families. Everyone knew that commuting every day by train was not easy. They were like single soldiers living in a brick building, escaping every weekend.

'At least you persuaded your wife!' Hyuk's colleagues were jealous. Eunwoo was still young. Third grade. Eunwoo's younger sister, Lia was only two. Eunwoo would adjust to a new school. Their new town wasn't actually that bad. The more the family explored, the more they liked it. And Eunwoo wanted to be close to his dad.

'We can bike and skateboard every night here, Hyuk said' The river was close. The park was huge. A half-hour drive took them to the beach. The amenities around the town were great for families. The city had been planned with quality of life in mind.

'Come to us,' the new city actively enticed potential families.

'Okay, let's move when our rental contract is up.' Nari had finally changed her mind. She also realized that they could buy their own house in the new city. They wouldn't have to rent any more. That excited her.

'We wouldn't need Ocean Blue,' Hyuk joked.

Nari grinned at him. 'Why?'

'Here we are surrounded by cement. This suffocates us. No natural air. No natural breeze. When we live near the beach, we won't have such problems.'

Staring at Ocean Blue, Nari nodded slightly. She agreed with Hyuk. *When we move, we can sell it second-hand online. It still looks so new. It's perfect!* She was content.

Two weeks passed. Hyuk came back home late. He had missed the usual train and had had to take the next one. He had told Nari to go to bed first, as he might not make it at all. He hadn't wanted her to wait up for him. He snuck into the house. It was already late. He tip-toed through the entryway. Everyone was sleeping in the living room. After he had started staying in the dormitory, the rest of the family had picked up the habit of sleeping together in the living room. They bundled together and fell asleep. The scene made him sad. Two months left. Actually, six weeks. He crawled over to them and tried to pat the kids. Rhythmic wheezing came out of his wife and both kids. It was a hoarse wheeze when they breathed out. He stroked his daughter's hair. Lia's lips seemed blue.

Is it because of the reflection of the moon through the window? In the silence, he only heard the whirring of that machine and his family's rough breathing. *Is it because of the humidifier?*

He checked on Eunwoo. Each intake of breath ended in a whistle. Eunwoo seemed to be gasping for air. Again, pale skin and blue lips. Hyuk approached the humidifier and turned it off. The blue glow disappeared. He drew in a breath, and the bleach-like smell poked his nose. He promptly scowled. He peered down at the kids' faces again. Careful not to wake them, he used the LED light on his keychain to inspect them. He tried not to direct the light into their eyes. It would wake them up. No movement at all. He hesitated a little bit. But he directed the light to their faces. Still, nobody moved. He checked one and then the other. It baffled him. He shook Nari gently. She didn't open her eyes. *Is she in a deep sleep?* He shook her more vigorously. Her eyes opened and then closed. He panicked. He shook the kids awake. He dialled emergency services.

★★★

Hyuk sat next to Nari's hospital bed when she began to stir. He watched her. Relief and dread washed over him at the same time. And jealousy—she didn't know the world had fallen apart.

Hyuk peered into her face. Her eyes would open, and she moved her mouth. But that was all. He had a tube running from under his nose to an oxygen tank, just as his wife had. Sitting next to her bed, he felt her fingers reach for his wrist. Nari made a move, but Hyuk responded, 'Easy, easy.'

'Where are our kids?' An unfamiliar husky voice came out of her mouth.

He held her hand in his two hands tightly. 'Keep sleeping. Everything is fine.' Despite his smile, Hyuk's voice shook slightly.

He put on a veneer of outward calm but inside was all tumult as he burned with frustration.

How could I not have noticed it? I should have been there . . .

'What happened? Are they okay?' Her eyes were desperate; her gaze fixed on his nose tube.

'Why do you have a tube on your face?' Her eyes were full of fear.

Hyuk smiled again and stroked her head. *I haven't lost her*. Her breathing was rough. He felt the pressure of her clasping his hand and then releasing it, as she drifted back to sleep.

Hyuk called the doctor. The doctor walked into the room. Young interns in white gowns followed quietly behind him. The slowness of the doctor's steps bothered Hyuk. *Was it from his confidence or indifference? Or maybe he sees her as just another miserable customer*, Hyuk thought. The doctor checked Nari and then looked at him. His eyes asked for permission. Hyuk slowly nodded. The doctor briefed them on the condition of her and the kids. He told them that their lungs had been attacked. The doctor used the word 'attacked'.

'Eunwoo is in the kids' section,' Hyuk added.

Nari struggled to speak. Hyuk could see her trying to cope with the pain. Lines appeared on her forehead. 'Where is she?' She was asking for Lia.

The doctor explained, 'You need a lung transplant. We are waiting for the call.'

Surprise flashed in her eyes. 'What about the kids?' Her breathing was laboured. She looked from Hyuk to the strangers in the white gowns.

'Take care of yourself first. Then we will talk,' the doctor told her. Hyuk exchanged awkward eye contact with the doctor.

The doctor was about to leave. She called to him, 'What happened to us?' She was nearly hyperventilating. The doctor was very careful . . . he was hesitating.

'We are trying to find the cause. The police sent someone to your house to check. They're checking for a gas leak or some other problem.'

His voice trailed off. 'I will be back in the afternoon.' He and the other white gowns started to march out. Hyuk needed immediate answers from the doctor. *Lung transplant? Do they get new lungs? From whom?* He would beg if he had to. Hyuk followed them and approached the doctor, demanding more information.

'Look,' the doctor turned to him with a sigh. 'His lungs are shutting down. We are going to need to take action.'

After speaking with the doctor, Hyuk understood that Eunwoo was in worse shape than his mother. Eunwoo couldn't breathe by himself. The hospital provided ECMO—whatever that was.

Hyuk had to make a decision while Nari was on painkillers. Eunwoo needed oxygen in his blood. Hyuk had never heard about ECMO in his life. *How can my son's life depend on my decision about an acronym I've never heard of?*

The doctor's face didn't conceal his concern as he told Hyuk that it was a machine that helped prevent respiratory failure. 'Before his brain is damaged, he needs help.' Hyuk had to make an immediate decision. He couldn't lose Eunwoo as well. He still hadn't told Nari about what had happened to Lia. It had been too late for her because her brain had already been affected.

'ECMO is not perfect. But at least we can hold onto him longer till we get a new lung.' Hyuk whimpered through the night, watching his son who woke from time to time and blinked slowly. Eunwoo's eyes filled with tears begging Hyuk for help.

★★★

May had been brutal to Sam Lee. His expertise was mergers and acquisitions. Several years earlier, when a deal had failed, he had been sent to take over this position. It had not been good from the start. He hadn't like it. His wife, however, had liked it because the position seemed stable. He didn't have to travel much. 'You will be in charge of a whole company,' she had said, beaming. *Let her believe that.* He hadn't bothered correcting her. She wanted to settle down near her parents.

At last, I made her happy.

That's how he tried to console himself. She still didn't know what was really going on.

But I'm Sam. A warrior.

In the first two years after Sam had taken charge, the firm had seen record profits. *I'm back*, he snorted.

That sort of success wasn't enough for Sam. Now, he was looking to leave the company. He knew that remaining the head of a local firm was a road to nowhere, even though it felt nice today. *This company is too small. The products aren't going to change anybody's life.*

So, he had interviewed with a global IT firm. His achievements had impressed them. The combination of documented skills in management and M&A made him attractive. Sam thought he should be involved with a higher-impact industry. He requested double his current salary, plus stock options. He felt that he was getting back on track after this detour. The job involved looking for rising tech firms to acquire. Government money was backing the firm under the surface. It couldn't go under. So much money was involved . . . many inventors and small companies with brains will be swallowed. Sam relished the thought of returning to the hunt. He knew he would get the job. 'As long as this stupid scandal passes,' he grunted to himself. He was almost out of the door.

His next move would be to implicate the former boss of the company. He was the asshole who had marketed the product in the first place. The report that had come in the day before showed 300 deaths and several thousand patients hospitalized. *Damn, the number is growing too quickly. I have to get out of this stinking business as soon as possible.*

Sam left the house early and headed to the office. *The earlier I get there, the better.* As the office building came into view, he saw that protesters had already gathered at the entrance. Of course, he didn't want to stand up to such noisy protesters.

'Use the side parking lot,' he instructed the driver. He had to avoid these people. They had brought banners. And the posters with photos were getting bigger. Pictures of children hooked up to oxygen tanks.

'Murderer' stood out in red letters in some Halloween-inspired font. Maybe his face would feature on the posters soon.

Why do all these Koreans take to the streets? Write to your incapable legislators! Form consumer advocacy groups.

All this drama . . . these people love drama too much.

Feeling frustrated, Sam shifted the blame here and there. He hadn't known about what had been going on when he had taken the position. And he hadn't really bothered to find out. The board was useless.

Lawyers, the right lawyers, were the ones he could turn to. He had taken the whole day off so he could have a strategy meeting with expensive lawyers that the company had hired. The lawyers must be waiting in the office now. They should have come up with some clear ideas for how the company could avoid taking too much damage from this scandal. More to the point, they should have a proposal for how he could get out of this unpleasant situation. That was their speciality after all.

Sam just wanted to move on. He had one foot out the door already. The company's complex structure would make it difficult to nail down anyone for those deaths and lung failures. *It will be a long fight.* One thing he clearly knew now was that he should jump ship before the problem grew larger.

Entering the building by the back entrance, he easily avoided the protesters on his way to the office. He marched in to find five lawyers sitting with cups of coffee in front of them in the meeting room.

As soon as Sam had joined this firm, he had renovated this executive meeting room. A new coffee machine from Italy sat in the room, boasting both functions. You could make coffee with easy capsules, and you could also enjoy high quality espresso with freshly ground coffee beans. Sam believed that a meeting room was the face of the company. The cost of renovation had been covered easily by the thousands of humidifiers he could sell because of the space. He knew that colleagues joked behind his back that he was only there to create his own café. He scoffed at them, those fools who thought just working long hours was enough—their asses glued to their seats. They didn't understand efficiency. They didn't know that a good cup of coffee in a satisfying space was part of making serious money.

When Sam entered the meeting room, the lawyers stood up. The lenses in their boss's rimless glasses glinted, reflecting the sunlight coming through the floor-to-ceiling window. The reflection covered his eyes, but Sam could see them smiling. It was a good sign.

Things will pan out.

Chapter 6
Mini

August 2001

'Mini will be with us always.'

She is shattered.

'She is a true angel.'

She evaporated.

'She saved so many lives.'

She was torn.

Jihoon looked around. It was Jihoon who had wanted to meet them all, but now he had regrets. *I shouldn't have come today.* It was too painful to see them. His heart twisted. All of them wore serious faces. They prayed, following the priest. In this moment, what religion you believed in was not important.

'She brought terrible sadness to us. But at the same time, she showed her courage.'

The priest stared at Jihoon. Jihoon could feel the weight of his gaze, requesting to be met. Jihoon didn't want that. He looked, nonetheless.

'I know your sadness. I know your misery. Jihoon, I hope you go beyond sadness. See what she did . . . they are all your children.'

Jihoon gazed back. What the priest said struck him.

'It is rare to have them all agree to see you. They wanted to share their thanks with you. They wanted to make sure you know . . .'

'Mini will be with us always.'

She is still here

'She is a true angel.'

She is the angel of these children.

'She saved so many lives.'

She lives in them.

Jihoon still didn't take his eyes from the priest. Jihoon started smiling. His face was transfigured with something like joy, sudden joy. Again, he looked around. Each family met his eyes. Finally, they became real. Jihoon was able to see each face. He could feel their deep gratitude. He could feel their relief, their sympathy for him. He walked over to each family. He held their hands. He hugged them. They were crying together.

You are my family. You are taking care of my Mini.

★★★

May 2001

'I don't see much of a future.'

There were several faces on Jihoon's screen. *Damn, his voice is important.* Jihoon had somehow felt that Jack would show more concern than others about this investment. So, this wasn't a flying start.

'I think they are a little bit disorganized because they still don't see their own potential. But I think if we give some directions to them, they might be promising.'

A few guys on the screen nodded. Julia raised her hand. 'I agree with Jihoon. We saw the food crisis several years back in Africa and the Middle East.'

'Did Darjil contact you, Jihoon? Did they say they will join the investment?'

A big name . . . that's why you are stuck, Jack. That's why you can't have your own jet yet.

Jihoon smiled with confidence. 'Not yet, Jack. But they will contact me within three days. They need to follow their procedures. And the headquarters is off on holiday. They are having a seventy-year anniversary party for the company. The executives will have to recover from that.'

Jihoon's arm kept getting pulled. He had to switch the hand he was using. He tried to avoid taking his eyes from the screen. But he couldn't help it. Mini was frowning and nearly in tears.

Jihoon patted his daughter's shoulder and scribbled something down on a piece of paper that Mini was using. He leaned so he wasn't visible on screen and whispered, 'Wait. Just ten more minutes! I promise!'

Jihoon turned to face the screen with a big smile and told the faces on it, 'I already asked them to prepare the second presentation for us—with the exact projections of profits over five years. I told them a ten-year projection for profit is too long for us.' He hoped five years would sound fine.

These greedy speculators couldn't even wait for two years.

'Shall we have a meeting next Friday? I'll make sure the Darjil boys attend.' Jihoon distracted them with Darjil and the tactic, of course, worked.

They all nodded. 'Sure, let's do that. You made a good point, Jihoon. Projections of profit for three to five years would be great. We don't want to wait too long. But we want to invest in something exciting and contribute to sustainability.'

At least Julia is being helpful, although sometimes she backs off in the end. Jihoon knew how to handle this Ivy-League educated, young, and rich crowd. Their vanity made it easier.

'Okay, then I will get back to you before next Monday about the schedule. Adios, friends.'

His fingers were hurried as they touched the screen to hang up. But he kept a big smile on his face till the faces were gone.

It was a nice day. *What a view.* From the café window, they could see people line up for bungee jumping. They were bungee jumping right above a herd of cattle. It should be called diving for cows. It was hard to understand the concept. Do people really like throwing themselves towards cows? It must be stressful for the cows.

Jihoon made eye contact with Mini immediately. The sweet potato bread and the apple bread were untouched.

'Mini, I thought that you would walk around. I said only ten minutes.'

The café had a massive amount of space. There was a zone with machines for picking up dolls and some Pokémon game booth.

'It was an hour, daddy. Not ten minutes.'

Mini had an unhappy look on her face.

Jihoon frowned and checked his watch.

Oops . . .

One hour had already passed.

Jihoon felt guilty. Seri had warned Jihoon to not use his phone on this trip.

★★★

'See what your daughter thinks about you.'

In Mini's drawings, there was no daddy. She had told the teachers that his best friend was his phone. Jihoon's clients and business partners were in different time zones. It led him to keep abnormal work hours. It sometimes happened that he wouldn't see Mini for several days.

'You need to take two days off. And travel with Mini. She wants to see the sea and blue sky with her dad. Dad and daughter only time!' Seri had also needed some 'me' time. Everything had been arranged by her.

★★★

Jihoon had promised Seri to stay off his phone, but he hadn't kept his promise even for a day.

'Oh . . . you didn't want to look around and check out the cows? Did you finish your ice cream?'

'You can't eat ice cream for an hour, daddy.' She looked unsatisfied. 'Cows don't talk. Staring at them for several minutes is enough.'

Jihoon was embarrassed and changed the topic.

'Did you use all the coins?'

'Yes.' Mimi's lips puffed out. 'No luck . . . no doll. No Pokémon cards . . .'

Jihoon smiled at Mini. *This city girl . . .*

Mini continued, 'You know how funny cows are. They stroke your hair with their mouths. They smile at you if they think you are their friend.'

Mini looked down at the paper.

'I was a little bit scared to be there alone.'

Jihoon saw the paper. Mini had actually drawn a very nice group of cows on the paper. Jihoon's ugly writing, asking for more time, had ruined her piece.

'Oh . . . sorry, dear. It was an important call. I will make it up to you. Let's walk around. And we can go to a restaurant. That restaurant provides the longest oarfish.'

'Uh . . . that sounds gross.' Mini winced.

'You know Mommy always finds the best restaurants when we travel. This is on Mommy's list!' Jihoon tried to sound excited. 'The fish is really long. The chef makes a nice dish with it.'

'Then, a lot of bones? Oarfish has so many little bones. I need Mommy to take those out.'

Jihoon laughed when he saw the fear on his daughter's face. He ruffled Mini's long hair.

'No. This restaurant has a special warrior against bones. A guy with two forks who can remove them all.' She put her arms together.

'A warrior?' Her eyes widened and reflected curiosity.

'Yep . . . a delicate warrior who can remove even the tiniest of bones swiftly.'

Jihoon winked and packed Mini's things. 'Let's go.'

We can't ignore such a nice day, he thought.

Mini smiled widely and they stood up from their chairs.

She was wearing a pastel rainbow-coloured dress. She had dyed each colour carefully with Seri. The seven pastel colours were a nice addition to a sunny day. Mini jumped around Jihoon. She then held her father's hand tightly. Jihoon smiled at her, feeling guilty.

He shouldn't have picked up the call. But Jihoon couldn't miss this chance. He was the mediator between venture capitalists and new entrepreneurs. This would be a good deal. Some still hesitated to invest big money in agriculture. But when agriculture combined with technology, it created a different story for speculators. Having grown up in the countryside, Jihoon knew this was not a good deal for the farmers. But it was the perfect chance for investors. Farming without farmers, farming with satellites, could be a brilliant idea to expand the yield of agricultural production. And at no human cost!

Jihoon had the foresight to sense that investors would gain a lot. People who don't know anything about education invest in education. Education is a safe zone. It never collapses. Agriculture, too. We have to eat. It's not a matter of farmers or producers any more. It's for the money. Jihoon was betting big this time, but he was confident. It was crazy to imagine satellites controlling what people grew, but he was sure that was the future.

The problem he faced now was that the brain guys were pure scientists and rookies. They had no idea what business was. He had been able to gather smart people from agriculture, engineering, and computer science, owing to his friend at university.

The speculators did not know the level of involvement Jihoon had in this business. The company was hurriedly set up. The first presentation had not impressed the venture capitalists. The young innovators still did not know how to sell themselves and their ideas.

Jihoon had not yet told Seri about this big investment. The last one had not yielded a nice outcome. This time, however, he was confident. It would push retirement up by ten years. Then he could spend time with Mini and Seri.

Thinking of their bright future, Jihoon headed to the parking lot with Mini. A café combined with entertainment, livestock, and a bit of nature had made this place popular. You could see the cows that give you the milk, yogurt, and ice cream in the café. This was like heaven for city people. No city noise, not many people and cars. The sky was amazing. It was not cut into by buildings. It was endlessly blue. Clouds floated above.

While they walked, Jihoon pointed out, 'Look at that! That looks like a dragon's head.'

Mini stared up at the cloud for a while. She wrinkled her brow. 'No, it's like a jumping lamb. Look at that! Short front legs . . .'

Jihoon laughed. 'Okay, you're right. It can be a jumping lamb.'

Jihoon used to love watching clouds. You could create interesting characters. As a child, when he took the school bus, that was what he enjoyed doing, making imaginary animals in the sky. Other friends got bored fast, but he did it for hours. After growing up, there was no time for the sky. No time to make imaginary friends.

It can be a good thing for me to do this with Mini. Finally, I find a friend I can cloud-watch with! Thinking of the fun he had in his childhood, Jihoon's lips automatically stretched into a smile.

Suddenly, the phone was ringing again. It was Tom. His future saviour, his money maker. Tom must be curious about the meeting Jihoon had just had. Jihoon had to tell him the presentation was locked in for two weeks later. Two weeks of preparation for the presentation in front of some new people as well as the previous crowd. That would not be a problem for Jihoon himself. The problem was that Tom and his team spent a lot of time in the lab and field, but not in the office on presentations. Jihoon had even had to teach them how to prepare each slide for their presentation. That had been painful. He felt that he had become their teacher, giving instructions every moment.

He had to pick up the phone. Tom would become paranoid if he didn't answer, thinking the meeting had not gone well. Just one minute. Tell him the meeting was fine, but he needed to prepare another presentation for a bigger jackpot. It would be a short phone call. The pastel rainbow was looking brighter.

Jihoon did not see the car speeding through the small parking lot. Mini was standing behind Jihoon, waiting for her dad, who was not moving. She called out for him, but Jihoon was busy putting earphones into his ears and then saying hi to Tom. Jihoon walked fast, grabbing his car keys at the same time.

Don't let him speak first. When Tom is nervous, he talks endless nonsense. Jihoon did not have time to boost Tom's confidence.

'I don't have much time, Tom, but everything is great.'

Switching the phone to his left hand, Jihoon accidentally dropped the car keys in the grass. *Damn it.* When he hurriedly kneeled to pick up the keys, he heard a shriek. A high-pitched shriek. He sprang up and spun around.

Where is Mini?

Jihoon's brain went numb. She was gone. She was not behind him. He saw only a pretty rainbow flying through the sky before diving to the ground, landing softly.

Chapter 7
Family

May 2002

'We are family.'

The priest started in a low, but peaceful voice. Jihoon took a sip of mint tea. The tea itself was fragrant, but the water was not hot enough.

'You did a glorious thing,' said the lady sitting next to Jihoon. She was very close to him. He didn't like it.

Did I do something glorious?

'We all went through difficult times, but we knew what was best for our loved ones. But we also need to console each other. We also should know what glorious work we did.'

Jihoon glanced at the priest. *He was the one who uses such words. 'Glorious work?'*

'When we share our experiences, we will continually remember what we did.'

The lady next to Jihoon thrust herself forward and suddenly grabbed his arm. 'He saved five angels' lives.'

Jihoon anxiously pulled his arm back from her hand. She didn't seem to mind. She raised her tone higher. 'He is such a hero.'

People smiled warmly at him. He avoided their gaze and took a sip of mint tea. The taste had gotten worse. Tepid water with mint was the worst. His favourite tea had somehow become the most disgusting tea in this place. He wanted to storm out. Their smiles made it seem like they were gloating.

'I brought home-made rice cakes.' The sappy lady next to Jihoon suddenly stood up. Her gesture seemed to anticipate Jihoon's next action. It was exaggerated.

They were sitting in a bright room within the church compound. To get there, Jihoon had followed the priest down a dark corridor. From the expansive main hall of the cathedral, they had walked down a cramped corridor hidden in the back. The more one walked down the corridor, the narrower it felt. Jihoon had expected to reach an even darker space at the end of the walk.

A door opened in front of him. Surprisingly, it was connected to a sunny, spacious room. The sun revealed a garden through the large windows.

The priest said the church grew produce for the priests and nuns. It was a special space. It took time for Jihoon's eyes to adjust to the light. It was a cozy place indeed. Jihoon could see that people worked hard to maintain it. There was even a good coffee maker. Around twenty people had gathered there. Most were ladies, and there were three men who had seemed to come with their wives. The energetic lady had certainly used the whole space. Rushing here and there, she moved a table in the middle and opened her bright blue bag. In her excitement, she was even humming lightly.

'You didn't like the word *glorious*.' A tiny woman stood next to Jihoon.

Jihoon had not even known she was standing there. Her white hair was carefully brushed and tied behind her head. Maybe her well-groomed hair made the opposite impression the rice-cake provider had made on Jihoon. Or her careful gestures and the soft tone of her voice relaxed him. Jihoon automatically—albeit slowly—smiled.

She offered him a plate with a small piece of rice cake. 'The lady is noisy, but her cake is the best of the best. She orders rice from her hometown and makes the cakes from scratch.'

The tiny woman gently pushed the plate into Jihoon's hands. The cake didn't look like rice cake.

It was a pumpkin-coloured round cake. Sprinkled with yellow bean powder on the edge, the pumpkin-coloured cake was in the shape of a heart. The rice-cake baker was busy distributing her cakes. Her gestures were big and exaggerated while her cakes were delicately made.

'You might not be interested but trust me. Try a little bit. It goes surprisingly well with coffee.'

Jihoon took the plate. He was still standing awkwardly. She sat in her seat and looked up at Jihoon with a gentle smile. Jihoon finally settled in his chair.

'In the beginning, I also felt very offended by the way they talk about us. We did something glorious? I don't want to be praised for what we did. I don't want glory.' Watching Jihoon settle down in the chair, the woman continued.

'But I started understanding . . . Before this centre started, we all made a difficult decision and let them spoil what remained of our loved ones. After that difficult decision, what we saw next was a flurry of white-gowned people acting like greedy zombies or hungry vultures. They took what they needed. And then that was it. After that, the rest of their bodies were dumped like garbage. No respect. Not even a respectful time was given to us to bid an appropriate farewell.'

She blushed. After an awkward moment, she sought a distraction from the topic. She looked over towards the coffee machine. The crowd had dispersed. She smiled at Jihoon and said cheerily, 'It's finally our turn.' She put her plate on her seat and walked over to the coffee machine. A grey-haired man was operating the machine. They nodded to each other. Then they talked. They seemed to talk about Jihoon but did not even glance in his direction. After a short exchange, the man busied himself with the coffee gadgets. His hands were swift and showed that he knew what he was doing. The grey-haired barista impressed Jihoon. He handed two cups of coffee to her. She brought them to Jihoon.

'After the gentleman lost his wife, he brought his coffee equipment to the centre and became our barista for when we get together. Sometimes, we have a small gathering with him. People who like his coffee and who want to have some quiet time come . . . you can join us too. His wife loved his coffee. Every cup he makes for us is from his heart.'

Jihoon took a sip of coffee. He turned his eyes to the gentleman. He could see he was really enjoying making each cup of coffee. The burst of steam from the coffee machine actually comforted Jihoon too.

'Start with this mild black coffee. Then you can go to a darker one! It is the best coffee for the first shot!'

Jihoon finally opened his mouth. 'I was able to say goodbye to my daughter in a good manner.' He had been thinking about what she had said.

She smiled. 'That's good. That's what this centre did. Many people regretted the decision they'd made after they saw how their family members were treated after the operation. They were shocked and devastated. They thought that they had made a difficult but good decision. But the day of the operation had been a nightmare for most. Many devastated families started coming out and discouraging other families who were about to make the same decision. But people here knew that what we had done was right. We didn't want to discourage people. Instead, we tried to talk to the hospital and bureaucracy. Respect us. Respect our decision and let us have time to say goodbye before we bury our family member.'

Jihoon had a bite of the rice cake. The texture was amazing. It melted on his tongue nicely, not like those overwhelmingly sweet pastries. He drank a sip of coffee as she looked on, encouraging him to try it.

'Then they changed their manners. They had been busy transferring what they had taken from our beloved and moving their parts to different hospitals.

They realized they had been like vultures . . . they had to do their work well and fast. So, now, at least, they give us time to say farewell to our family members and help us collect their bodies and hold a funeral in a dignified way.' She then took a deep breath, taking in the aroma of her coffee and exchanged a smile with the barista. She waited till Jihoon was done enjoying the rice cake and coffee.

'That's why we try to console ourselves by saying we did a glorious thing.' She continued, 'Although the situation has improved now, we still need time to digest the situation or time to justify things to ourselves. Anyway, we are the ones who are left in this world.' She stopped and stared at the rice cake for a while.

'The lady who made this cake had very hard time,' she went on. 'She lost her son. She didn't know the son had entered this agreement before passing away. He had done it when he was in military service. Maybe at that time he didn't know this could be his story. But he obviously had good intentions.

'Then when he died in an accident while in the military, she and her family got to know about what he had agreed to. Her parents-in-law and husband were from an old-fashioned town. A strong Confucian family—quite a famous family in their hometown.

They were furious. They couldn't agree. A transplant is basically destroying your body . . . and that, to them, meant he couldn't go to heaven. He couldn't have an appropriate funeral. That's what they believed. They blamed her for poisoning him with bad ideas. They just needed some target for their anger and despair.'

Jihoon looked at the cake lady. She was still busy distributing her rice cakes and packing some for people to take home. She was all smiles.

'But she insisted. She said that's what her son wanted to do. Of course, divorce followed. She received nothing from thirty years of marriage.

'After she said goodbye to her son, she hit rock bottom. When she entered this centre, her eyes were completely empty and gosh . . . she was so skinny . . . like a walking skeleton.'

It was hard to believe her when Jihoon glanced at the cake lady again. The lady was full of life. No one would believe she had such a horrible past.

'The centre changed her. People consoled her and recommended her to learn something. We realized she had a singular aptitude for baking and crafts. That's who she is now.'

Jihoon stared at her. He suddenly felt bad for immediately hating her.

'She has her own cake shop now. One of the centre people let her use a small space from their building. She could attract many people with her rice cakes.'

Jihoon stared at the remaining bit of rice cake on his plate. 'Yes, I can see why people love these cakes.'

'She brings them every time she comes to our meetings.'

The two ladies made eye contact. The cake lady raised more cakes towards the white hair lady. The white hair lady smiled back and shook her head. 'She doesn't have to come here all the time. Her business thrives. But she never forgets to feed us.'

Jihoon finished his cake. It was the perfect amount of sweet. Not excessive. Not artificial. Jihoon felt that he needed that sweetness . . . natural sweetness from real love.

He finally opened his mouth. 'I had my daughter back after the operation. The hospital even introduced morticians. They did such a good job. So, I thought that's how it had always been . . . I didn't know what this centre did.'

'Come and meet us regularly. We don't talk much about our pain. It's always in the beginning . . . but anytime you would like to talk about it, come to us. We understand what you are going through. The people here are nice. And like I said, we know what you are going through. We *are* you.' She patted Jihoon's shoulder. His mother would probably be her age if she were still alive. Her soft tone shook Jihoon's heart and cooled his anger.

'I had the opportunity to meet so many families. I saw their kids overcome illness. I saw them return to normal life . . . I can still see Mini in them.' Jihoon smiled. Jihoon was about to say more about those kids. He expected some response from her. Instead, her face looked a little bit wistful. Her response was quite unexpected.

She stared at Jihoon silently for a moment. She took another sip of coffee. 'All family members,' she repeated, musing, and asked Jihoon, 'they can reach you?' She wanted to make sure one more time.

Jihoon nodded. *Was something wrong?*

She furrowed her brow slightly. It was hardly noticeable, but Jihoon caught it. She slowly opened her mouth.

'That's nice . . . that's nice.' She looked into Jihoon's eyes. 'Hm . . . but if I can dare to say, I recommend you to—and I know it is hard, but you should focus on yourself from now on. Contacting them is good but you should make a decision someday soon that you will say goodbye to them and have physical distance.'

She shifted in her seat and sat up straighter. 'It's good for you. I mean, of course you won't forget Mini. She will be with you forever. But what I'm saying is that make space in your heart. Have your own full life and take care of the family with you now. It might take time . . . your pain will never completely leave. But it will wear away as time goes by. I hope that you can soon say bye to them and get your own full life back. If you are still around them, the pain will linger.'

Jihoon stared at her. He didn't like what she had said. She'd never seen Mini. Although she'd also gone through the same procedure with one of her family members, Jihoon felt that she didn't understand either.

Jihoon would find out much later that she had been right.

Chapter 8
Debt

27 February 2010

'Did you recognize him right away?'

Young brought some salted anchovies and roasted peanuts.

'You said I can't have food after 7,' said Minsu, his eyes wide open.

Six months earlier, Young had announced firmly to her husband, 'After dinner, the kitchen is closed!'

Tonight, it was Young's turn to do to the dishes. When Minsu had come out of the shower room, he had seen the dishes arranged on the dining table. Young, standing in front of the table, had been waiting till Minsu came out.

Young said, 'Tonight is special . . . just thinking about old times . . .'

She then turned towards the refrigerator and took two bottles of beer out. *It is a special night.* They were silent for a moment.

'Where had you hidden these anchovies? I know you hid them so I couldn't find them.'

Minsu smiled at Young. Young had been worried about Minsu's belly.

What can I do? This is the evidence of a hard-working middle-aged man. Minsu suddenly thought about Jihoon.

'It took time because of his silver hair. Except for that, he was unchanged.'

Jihoon looked fit. Ten years had passed. His hair had turned white. Except for that, he looked like someone who had spent time taking care of his appearance. Minsu looked down at his bulging belly while holding a bottle of beer. *I should really stop drinking.*

Young took a sip of beer and tossed peanuts into her mouth. 'I know. The first time I looked at him, I thought, "Who is this guy?" I thought a middle-aged actor had moved into our neighbourhood. Such a knockout.'

Young saw Minsu's jealous eyes.

As Minsu showed his indifference to her comment, he gulped his beer down. Young smiled at him and lowered her eyes to the flower bowl full of anchovies and peanuts. *They don't match . . . flowers and twisted dry anchovies.*

Again, they sipped their beer in silence. *Of course, we understand . . .*

'He seems all right now and even smiles. We didn't see that before.'

'Yeah . . . I know . . . he smiled once when he approached us and held our hands. Do you remember what he said at that time?'

'How can I forget?' Minsu finished the bottle. He reached for a second beer. Young moved her hand to slow him down, then retreated.

Young responded with her own questions. 'Why do you think he suddenly showed up? Do you think it is a coincidence?'

Minsu was focused on his second bottle. Young leaned in to regain his attention.

Minsu looked away, towards the living room. 'I don't think so. I don't know . . .'

'You know he is already famous here. All the ladies talk about him.'

Minsu chuckled. 'Yeah? Why?' He returned his gaze to hers.

Minsu caught Young's sparkling eyes with excitement.

'Because of his appearance?' Minsu's jealousy returned.

'Besides that, I heard from our neighbours that he is a single.'

Minsu raised his eyebrows in surprise.

'What? Where is his wife?'

He also acknowledged he had not seen her at all when Jihoon was busily walking around and organizing his new house.

'I don't know. What I heard from them was that he is a single guy and he is wealthy. He bought the house on the spot. You know real-estate people; they are the source of gossip. Without any negotiation, he just walked into Ms Chang's office and grabbed the house like a child takes his favourite candy. He just used his phone and transferred the entire payment at the asking price in five minutes.'

'You know Ms Chang exaggerates about prices, too. I'm sure she's doing it again this time. To push the price up around here.'

While Minsu was lightly responding to Young, he felt jealous. They were still having hard time to pay back the loan for this house. After moving more than ten times, they had finally settled down in this house. They knew that this residential district and the property were beyond their means. But they wanted Gun to live in a house, not in a match box. Gun might have some side effects later. He had not shown any noticeable symptoms. But being close to the ground and to the soil would be better for him. So, they made a bold decision. This would be their permanent home. This new community would be their root! No more moving in and out. They were happy with the house and a small yard. The low fences of neighbouring houses were perfect. They trusted each other. Although they were happy, they were still paying more than they could afford to the bank. Young felt bad for Minsu for that. She quit her job after Gun's episode. After he goes to university, then perhaps she would look for a job. Maybe she wouldn't have to check his medicine box any more.

Young wanted to talk more about Jihoon. Light gossip was the best distraction from her worries. 'Ms Chang told us that he has so much cash. He came back from Singapore and had been in finance. She was saying he owns buildings in Gangnam. He doesn't even have to work. She couldn't stop talking about him. How wealthy he is and how he has no affectation . . . his manners are great.'

Minsu put a bunch of anchovies in his mouth and chewed them very nervously.

Wasn't he a workaholic? There was gossip that it was his fault he had lost his daughter. No one dared to ask. Everyone was busy taking care of their own business. But what they heard was that's why they didn't see his wife at that time when they had gathered.

What irony. A tragedy for one created happiness for others.

Minsu was about to spit out the anchovies, but he swallowed them. *Come on, we owe him so much.*

Minsu changed the topic. 'A funny thing was that he recognized us right away and even remembered Gun's name.'

Young got closer to Minsu. 'Did you also think it was odd? It was odd. He seemed to know about us well. The way he was talking to us and asking questions about Gun was like he has been around all the time.'

'Yeah . . . that was peculiar.'

'I remember after we met him the last time, and he said at that time he would travel for a while. When was that? Was it six months after the surgery?'

'About that,' Minsu thought out loud.

Young saw Minsu's gloomy face. When Jihoon had suddenly disappeared from their lives, they were shocked. And they were relieved. There was some guilt whenever they saw Jihoon. With him gone, they were able to move on.

Young brought more anchovies.

'Anyway, those difficult times passed. It is odd we have run into him again. But maybe it is nothing. Maybe it shows we made the right choice!'

Young gulped her beer.

'Owing to him, the value of this community went up! A successful rich guy bought a property like that.'

Young suddenly clapped her hands. She was getting into a good mood. 'Oh! Honey, you know what . . . some neighbours say we should set him up with Jina.'

Minsu smiled and blushed. A humdrum community looked for a little excitement, and they finally found their target.

'What? The woman living in the house with the red roof? No no . . .'

'Why not? She has high standards, she's just divorced. A beauty in this area. She always talks mixing English that nobody understands.' Young's face brightened at the idea of setting this up.

'Don't be involved, Young. We don't know how he thinks.'

'Surely not, I'm just saying his appearance made these neighbours lively. Suddenly we have this idol here, a silver-haired idol. Idols don't have to be kids in their early twenties. We also want some romance. In reality, we're all spoken for, but we can still fantasize about romance at our age. He enlivens our prosaic daily routines. He definitely brought a fresh wind here.' Young was embarrassed to speak like this to Minsu but nonetheless continued talking like an excited teenager. There was a shy smile on her flushed face.

Minsu was laughing. Young was glad to see his mood improve. She had felt perplexed when they had run into Jihoon and hadn't known how to react. But maybe it was time for them to pay back their debt to him a little. She understood why his wife was not with him and felt sad. They might have been apart right after that. It was good to see him in perfect shape and healthy. His well-being made her happy, although there was some checking to do. Otherwise, she would have been wondering about his whereabouts till she died.

Suddenly thinking about these matters, Young felt strongly motivated to introduce Jina to Jihoon, without letting Minsu know, of course. Many neighbourhood ladies didn't like Jina because of her pretentious elegance. Even the way she walked was pretentious. Young knew the ladies would sarcastically say that Jina was finally in her own league, but they didn't mean it. No one wants their idol *oppa* to be taken by another woman. But Young thought Jina's lively and positive personality could be good for Jihoon.

The night got darker. They waited for Gun to return from school. Night study should be finishing soon.

'Please take care of my Mini.' Jihoon's final words to them in the past, which he'd said while holding their hands, echoed in Minsu's mind as he finished the second bottle. *Why does his sudden appearance bother me so much? We are grateful to him.* Minsu blamed himself. *What kind of horrible human am I?*

Chapter 9
Heart: Mackerel

June 2001

It started with a stomach ache.

They had had a nice dinner. Minsu's mother had sent mackerel from a famous fishing town. The deliveryman handed them to Young. When Young heard the bell ring, she opened the door. The deliveryman had disappeared, and she heard the elevator shut. In front of the door, a Styrofoam box was waiting for Young. She dragged the box from the corridor into the flat. The ice inside gave it its weight. When she opened the box, a white fog oozed out of the box and spread through the apartment. Young dug through the nuggets of dry ice to find the pieces of mackerel, frozen solid. Their dead eyes reflected the chill of the icy box.

Young called her mother-in-law to thank her.

'They are fresh. Enjoy.'

She had made sure the frozen mackerel had been recently caught. It was her way of expressing love for her son and grandson. She knew how much her grandson Gun liked mackerel.

'So much like his dad. Even his taste comes from his dad.' Young's mother-in-law of course liked the idea that her son and grandson had the same taste. Minsu cooked a few of the fish while Young prepared the bean curd soup, the perfect accompaniment to mackerel. She had just bought kimchi from the street market. It was the Jeolla version, Minsu's favourite, with a stronger seafood flavour.

They had a good dinner. A good meal could make anyone happy. They were focused on eating and complimenting the baked mackerel. The conversation naturally moved to Gun's grandmother. Minsu was glad to hear how excitedly Gun talked about Grandma and her house. He wanted to go visit her immediately once the school vacation started. Grandma was Gun's best friend. The family was content. Young was not as excited as Minsu or Gun. A trip to Grandma's meant that she had to follow Gun for two months, while Minsu enjoyed life as a single man in Seoul, on the pretext of work. Young's job was good. As a teacher, she too enjoyed school vacations. But that also meant she had another job—one as a daughter-in-law—for the weeks she stayed with Minsu's mother. Young was thinking of applying for an extra administrative job at the school. If she were given the role of planning the school curriculum in the summer, her duties as daughter-in-law would diminish. She felt guilty about her idea, but she needed her own break after teaching. At least she could make a good excuse as to why she had to stay in Seoul. And there would be extra money too. Gun had no choice then but to stay in Seoul as well.

Minsu and Gun headed to the bathroom to brush their teeth, after watching their favourite reality comedy show.

'My belly hurts,' Gun complained.

'Did you eat too fast?'

Minsu put the toothpaste on his and Gun's toothbrushes. Minsu didn't take the complaint seriously. Gun didn't want to go to bed. Resting on the sofa, he wanted to continue watching TV. *So, he is making an excuse, saying he has a bellyache.* Minsu turned the TV off, dragging Gun, who was still complaining, to bed.

An hour later, Gun came out of his bedroom. Having just turned off the light in the living room, Minsu and Young were about to go to bed.

'My belly hurts so much.' Gun was crying.

Young put him back to bed and stroked his belly. He didn't have a fever. He kept crying and squirmed in pain.

'Was the fish undercooked?' With worried eyes, Young looked at Minsu.

Minsu shook his head. 'No way, we cooked them thoroughly. You and I are fine.' Minsu was defensive. Blaming the mackerel seemed like blaming his mother. Young said nothing further.

Gun's bellyache persisted. Then it got worse. Young called her school nurse, apologizing for the late call. The nurse recommended that they take him to the hospital. 'It's strange. Maybe norovirus or food poisoning, and he is showing symptoms before you. I would check any available emergency room.'

In the middle of night, they hurriedly put on their jackets and took Gun to the emergency room.

'It seems to be enteritis,' the doctor said.

'But he hasn't had diarrhoea' Minsu answered with a puzzled face. Minsu had suffered from enteritis, and so he had become a semi-expert in the unpleasant disease. The doctor suggested a CT scan.

Carrying diarrhoea medicine, the family returned home. Gun's abdominal ache didn't go away. Minsu didn't defend his mother's present any more. He took the frozen mackerel out and smelled it.

He called his mom, checking where she'd bought them from. Nothing was unusual. The same place, the same delivery company.

Gun's illness worsened. They went to different clinics. They were asked the same question: 'What did you eat today?' and the conclusions were the same; it was enteritis. They stopped once more, this time at a university hospital.

A young ER doctor checked him. Hearing about Gun's nightmare journey through several clinics, she checked his heartbeat carefully. The other doctors had rushed to poke and prod Gun's belly.

She was not interested in Gun's abdomen.

'His heartbeat is abnormal.'

The doctor got to her feet and pushed the stethoscope back into her white gown. Minsu and Young gawked at the young girl. She used the internal phone. 'Please take one patient to the cardiac department. Yes. You'd better take him there.'

Cardiac department?

Half in disbelief, they followed Gun, who was being taken away by two nurses. The nurses had brought a wheelchair, and the wheels were moving faster than any normal bicycle.

It was not enteritis. The problem was in the muscles around his heart. Paediatric cardiomyopathy was the immediate diagnosis. A healthy boy had suddenly been diagnosed with a rare disease that Minsu and Young had never heard of.

'His heart muscles are abnormally enlarged.'

Minsu and Young tried to be patient. At least it was not enteritis. There must be a solution.

'It is rare . . . very rare.' The older doctor said 'rare' twice. *It does not sound good,* Minsu thought. The young doctor was standing next to him. She was serious, not showing a single expression. There was no satisfaction on her face about being right.

'It is a very rare heart disease.'

It was not about the mackerel. It was not about his intestines. It was about his heart. Minsu and Young could not have expected that at all. The young doctor, who looked like a teenage girl, had been right. Maybe she had saved Gun's life. But that was not the end of the story. His symptoms worsened, and it happened as suddenly as the initial stomach ache had.

'What did we do wrong?'

Minsu and Young wanted to understand. If it was not the mackerel, there had to be some other reason. But the doctors did not explain. They just suggested that Gun needed a heart transplant and immediately put his name on the waiting list. They received permission from Minsu and Young to use ECMO and made Gun fall asleep by putting a sleeping pill in the pipe. Minsu and Young tried to think hard about where they could have gone wrong. *Do we have any family members who have heart issues?* Being sick from mackerel sounded better now. They suddenly wanted to blame the young doctor, as if she had purposefully discovered something taboo or had knowingly opened a pandora's box.

He was a healthy boy. He had not been seriously sick before.

'Unfortunately, this happens. It is very rare. You did nothing wrong. It is not your fault.' The doctor tried to comfort them.

'Don't feel guilty. Try to focus on the next step. I have to be honest. It can be very tough. He needs to find a new heart. His heart will not function completely. ECMO has its limits, and he cannot fully depend on the machine. Time is ticking and he needs a new heart from someone who is of similar age.' The young doctor's voice became dimmer. 'That's the tricky part.'

Where do we find a fresh heart? Minsu and Young just stood and listened. There was a long silence.

They were trying hard to understand how a stomach ache had become heart failure. *We must be dreaming.*

Chapter 10
Deal

1 October 2010

Minsu stopped himself. He panted a little bit and turned his head towards a honking sound. It was Jihoon. Jihoon slid down the window of his car and gave a smile. Shiny white teeth welcomed Minsu.

'Minsu, are you walking back home?'

'Oh, hey. Yes. I am walking back.' It was a surprise for Minsu. He didn't want to run into any neighbours at the moment. The last person he wanted to meet was Jihoon.

'Hop in. I will take you home.' The door of the passenger seat opened smoothly and welcomed Minsu.

Minsu hesitated. He had promised Young that he would walk back home so he could get in some exercise every day. But he felt tired. Winter was coming. Minsu was already sweaty from walking.

And it was a Rolls-Royce. It was Minsu's, or every man's, dream car. If Young had been next to him, Minsu would have said no without hesitation. He wouldn't have wanted her to compare it to their own car. Unconsciously, Minsu looked around. No one was nearby.

'Thanks.'

Minsu hopped in the car. Sitting in the seat, he almost groaned. It was a new world. *What would I feel if I held the steering wheel? How soft would it be?*

He smelled a female fragrance in the car. *Strange.*

'But you should let me off near your house. So, Young won't see that I cheated on my exercise.'

'Ha, so that's why you were walking. I wondered whether your car had broken down.'

'No . . . I need to get rid of this beer belly.' Minsu felt more comfortable now. His stinky body got fresher in the car. He felt a little guilty wondering if his presence in the car would ruin the car seat.

'You know what? Since you moved in here, owing to you, the neighbourhood wives reprimand their husbands. They want their men to look like some kind of middle-aged idols. I have to thank you as a representative of the beer-belly men here.'

Jihoon laughed. 'Is that because of me? Then I should catch up with you guys. That would be faster.'

Jihoon confidently held the steering wheel with his left hand and patted Minsu's shoulder with his right. Minsu was slightly jealous of Jihoon's relaxed state. *When you have that much money, it probably comes naturally. Money and relaxation . . .*

'Are you making fun of us?' Minsu looked down at his paunch and patted it. He made his belly more bloated. He hated himself for making himself a clown, but he had done it before he could think twice about it.

Jihoon smirked. 'Ha ha. No, no. It is just a tropical zone thing. When you live in a tropical zone for several years, you sweat so much that it takes everything extra out of your body.'

'Hm. I don't buy it. My colleague lived in Malaysia for five years. When he came back, he was twice as big. We didn't even recognize him. We were worried about him. He said simply just as you, "It's a tropical zone thing."' Minsu lifted his shoulders. 'So, whom shall I trust? You or my colleague?'

Hearing Jihoon's laugh, Minsu leaned back in the seat. *This is heaven!*

'Okay, okay, sorry. I'm also chased by the ladies' kindness. People in this area are way too nice.' Jihoon's fingers followed the rhythm of the music in the car. Minsu saw the letters, 'pink martini' on the fancy media screen in the car. A female singer with a soft voice was calling a name: 'Eugene, Eugene.' *Hope someone would hum my name with such a sweet tone,* Minsu thought. He couldn't understand the lyrics, but he felt the song must be about missing the man named Eugene. Minsu was unconsciously calling his name too, following the singer. Jihoon seemed content to have a happy guy next to him too.

'Is that why there is so much fragrance in here?' Minsu hoped the drive home would be long enough to satisfy his curiosity.

Jihoon smiled at Minsu. 'I just got back from a blind date with a lady introduced to me by one of our community members.'

Minsu opened his eyes wide. 'Wow, so my deduction was right! That explains the fragrance and why you spruced yourself up. How did it go?'

Minsu didn't want Jihoon to feel like he was another nosy onlooker. But he was sure Jihoon could feel his excitement and curiosity.

'Ha, we just had dinner. And she was very nice.'

'So, you can drive slowly. This will be good information for Young.'

'I'm sure she already heard from Jina.' Jihoon seemed to catch how much Minsu enjoyed the car. He drove slowly.

'Oh! Jina! Wait a minute! Is Young the one who introduced you?'

Jihoon grinned. 'You guys are too nice to me.'

'I told her not to get involved in such a thing.'

'No, no. Please don't scold her. I'm sure she thought that's how she can help me. I really appreciate it. And, actually, I had a nice dinner with Jina.'

Minsu had initially been embarrassed, but now his curiosity grew. 'So, there will be another date?'

Jihoon's smile said no. 'I am so comfortable with my life now, and I don't want to go out with a neighbour, you know. I just want to be a nice neighbour, a nice uncle, and a nice gardener.'

'Wow, you rejected her. She must have been mortified.' Minsu laughed loudly.

Jihoon immediately refuted him. 'No, no. We were on the same page. We will have a meal together as friends—but not as dates—from time to time.'

Minsu looked at Jihoon. Several months had passed since Jihoon had moved in. Surprisingly, he had adjusted well. His house was big for one person. This new town on the outskirts of Seoul was designed for people who wanted to live in houses rather than match boxes in the city. Each house had a low fence, utterly unlike Seoul. The nearby highway onramp provided a quick connection to the city. It was not Seoul, but people who were sick of city life and had a little flexibility in their work hours started moving to these new types of towns. People trusted each other. Perhaps trust came from assumptions about status, knowing that you had to be able to afford the place. Minsu and Young had different reasons—reasons related to Gun's health. Their house was quite humble compared to their neighbours. They'd been lucky to get the house.

In contrast, Jihoon's house was fancy and elegant. The previous owner had not been able to find a buyer because of the price. It was a three-storey house that looked like a model European house and had big front and back yards. One of the developers must have been eager to live in such a fancy place, but even they had not been able not afford it. It had stood empty, but the developers had taken care of it because it was the face of the community. Finally, an owner was found in Jihoon after three years of vacancy.

Jihoon immediately made the house even more beautiful than the original. He started gardening, growing different coloured flowers. Several gardeners were hired. He also set up an indoor garden with glass all around. Jihoon looked like he knew what he was doing. Gardening gadgets were on display. He grew an interesting variety of vegetables, taking care to distribute samples to his neighbours. The green house became the attraction of the town. It looked like a tea house you'd see in photos of European country homes. He planted herbs in the indoor garden.

The neighbourhood ladies became more interested in gardening. They tried to get advice from him. Herbs were just not plants, apparently. He shared exotic recipes for how those herbs could be used. Italian, French, and other types of dishes could be made with herbs from his garden. He was surrounded by ladies who praised his sophisticated, cosmopolitan taste.

The men of the neighbourhood assumed Jihoon would have a haughty demeanour. However, he had turned out to be the opposite. His friendly manner quickly thawed the envy of husbands. The real-estate agent, Ms Chang, had not been bluffing in the end. Property prices in the district went up. Residents were happy. Husbands happily accepted him and started getting along with him. He let his neighbours feel like they were in his league. A big illusion, but not a bad one.

At first, when Jihoon knocked on the door of their house, they didn't recognize him at all. Young just looked at him with curiosity, wondering who this handsome gentleman was. Jihoon showed his surprise and asked whether they remembered him. It took them some time to remember. A long silence, and shock. Young's eyes changed immediately. Jihoon's happy face relaxed them later, and the awkward moment passed. Since that time, Jihoon had become a good neighbour.

But he never went beyond a certain limit. Jihoon was happy to see Gun and smiled warmly at him. Gun's indifference towards the new neighbour didn't bother Jihoon much. Gun simply started acknowledging Jihoon as a rich neighbour and saying hi to him.

Now, Minsu and Jihoon were sitting together in the car, and talking about a date. Minsu felt awkward and sad, thinking back to when they had met each other for the first time.

'Young will be disappointed. She thought that you and Jina would be a perfect couple,' Minsu said. 'Young told me Jina is knowledgeable, international, and outgoing.'

Jihoon grinned. 'Yep. She is! She is not timid.'

Minsu felt ill at ease and brushed his hair. 'You know many ladies kept asking why you are alone and saying you should find a perfect woman who suits you. Some neighbours have long tongues. Young seemed not to have a choice since our neighbours know we seem to know each other. I'm sure Young thought hard and decided Jina is the best match for you.'

Jihoon didn't respond right away. Then he said, 'After Mini, Mini's mom left me. We tried to get together once. But it didn't work. It was brief, but the pain was too much.'

Minsu was surprised. It was the first time Jihoon had talked about his wife. He knew Jihoon was not with her any more, but it was impossible to ask what had happened to her. They just knew he lived alone.

'She is far better now and happy. She married again and has a newborn son.'

Minsu didn't know what to say.

Jihoon seemed to read Minsu's discomfort. 'It's okay. It's water under the bridge.' He continued with a good countenance.

'I'm satisfied with my life now.' Jihoon looked at Minsu. 'I have you guys. I did enough in this life. I just want to enjoy small things—taking care of plants and veggies, travelling when I want. I already have many families whom I must take care of.'

Minsu couldn't completely understand what Jihoon meant. But he could sense Jihoon's pain.

'Jihoon, you are still attractive to the neighbourhood ladies. You are young and good looking. You seem to have everything. People in this town also like you. They won't let you be alone.' Minsu gave the slight warning to Jihoon since he knew the neighbours here. They loved these distractions.

Jihoon grinned and stretched his arms, his fingers tightening slightly on the steering wheel. 'I want to talk about other stuff. Since it is just you and I here now, Minsu. So, I have been thinking about this for a while. And I have waited for the right moment to ask.' He paused, and then continued, 'I would like to offer some financial contribution to Gun's education. If this is not acceptable, please tell me. It's absolutely fine for you to say no as his father. I know Gun wants to go to the Science and Technology University. It is very competitive. And the tuition fee is high.'

Minsu was a little flustered. Jihoon had suddenly changed the topic from himself to Gun.

Jihoon slowed the car further and said, 'I want to contribute to his tuition, and if he wants to study more later . . . like abroad I mean, then I can be like a financial guardian. Again, I'm just suggesting it. Gun doesn't have to know. You can talk to Young first.'

With an open mouth, Minsu looked at Jihoon.

Recognizing Minsu's face, Jihoon laughed briefly and continued, 'Minsu, you know me. I want Gun's future to be bright. I worked hard after what happened to my family. And I was lucky, I mean, in financial matters. I received more money than I need for myself. That is what I have been always good at . . . I wish it was the other way around, though.'

Jihoon paused, perhaps thinking about Mini.

'So, you can give Gun the best options. Nowadays, raising kids is an investment. Sadly, that is the reality. I don't like the reality, how crazily the world is changing. But we don't need to sugarcoat the reality.'

With a concerned face, Jihoon said, 'If it is uncalled for, please let me know. No pressure.'

'I don't know what to say . . . We already owe you so much . . .'

'Don't mention it. You guys are like my family. Gun is special to me.' Jihoon paused a little and checked Minsu's reaction awkwardly. He continued, 'Gun doesn't have to know about it. I just want to do a meaningful thing in my life.'

It had just been a car ride. Minsu had not expected this amazing offer. *Did Jihoon know about what was happening with my miserable and secret disaster?* Minsu's head was busy thinking about this moment and himself. He had lost big on the stock market again recently. He was determined to not invest in stocks any more. He had thought it would be the fastest way for him to retire. He was tired of the life of a salary man. The scanty income could not satisfy his family. He had pulled out a big chunk of his pension and it had turned into a disaster.

Or his drastic, stupid decision might have been because of Jihoon. Minsu had been following his example. Jihoon's financial success was not from hard work and from working for hours daily. A salary could not bring you financial freedom. Toiling in a company that you did not like was depressing. Everyone knew that, but everyone was afraid of falling out of the spinning wheel. Dreaming of being Jihoon, Minsu made an irrational choice. He thought his gamble had been calculated, but he had been reckless. He should have studied more before jumping in.

He couldn't be Jihoon. He could have at least asked Jihoon for some advice before investing. But his pride had deterred him. Minsu, deep down, blamed Jihoon, and he cursed him for appearing in this town. But now, Jihoon was about to extend a helping hand to Minsu and become his saviour. Gun's tuition fee would have become one major source of family debt, and sitting in that dream car, Jihoon's offer brought Minsu the hope of a fantastic world.

Minsu tried not to show his excitement. 'Thanks, Jihoon. This is a huge offer. I will discuss it with Young. I feel like I have gotten so much from such a short ride. This has been the luckiest hitchhike of my life.'

Jihoon showed his white teeth as he smiled. 'Ha ha. Please don't forget to tell Young I enjoyed dinner with Jina . . . as a friend. She is good company. Such a smart lady! She has a quaint sense of humour.' Jihoon seemed to know Minsu wouldn't refuse his generous offer.

'Jina? Oh, sure. Don't worry about that part.' Minsu had completely forgotten about Jina and Jihoon's date.

They parked the car in Jihoon's house.

'So . . . you should perhaps run a little bit now. Otherwise, Young will be suspicious, seeing you look fresh after the long walk.'

'That's a good point.' Minsu chuckled. He hopped out of the car. He was about to wave to Jihoon, when Jihoon interrupted him, having just remembered something. 'Oh, by the way, I am a little bit worried. It seems Gun spends a lot of time on his phone. Sometimes, he walks while watching the phone screen.'

He was talking yet again about Gun, but Minsu didn't mind. It actually made him smile. Jihoon already acted like a guardian. Jihoon continued, 'He spends quite a bit of time on the playground but is on his phone the entire time.' This was new information about Gun that Minsu had not known about.

Minsu winced at the comments. 'Does he? I know that phone is his best friend, but I didn't know he had such an unhealthy habit.' He was wondering to himself when Gun found time to spend at the playground. Was it when he came back from night study?

Jihoon tried to lighten the atmosphere. 'I'm not telling on him so don't say it was me. I know that's what teenagers do now. But there are also reckless drivers. That's why I wanted to share this with you so he can be careful before anything happens, you know.'

Jihoon couldn't finish his sentence, and Minsu caught the moment pain flashed in his eyes. He had to stop the conversation before it reminded Jihoon of the past.

'Okay. Don't worry about it. Thank you so much for letting me know. I will definitely take action.' Minsu studied Jihoon to check whether he was okay. Jihoon gave a thumbs up.

Minsu responded with a smile. 'Thanks again.'

Minsu started walking towards his house at a considerable pace. Halfway there, he turned his head back. Jihoon hadn't yet gotten out of his car. He sat there; eyes fixed on Minsu. Minsu waved to him, but Jihoon didn't respond, only staring at him. Minsu didn't mind. *Maybe this side is very dark. Jihoon can't even see me.*

As Minsu walked home, he kept telling himself, *Take this chance, Minsu.* He was attempting to silence any doubts. He seemed to have already made a decision about what he would tell Jihoon.

Chapter 11

Cornea: Modern Stigma

Late May 2001

'*Atopy*, from the Greek, *atopos*. Do you know what that means?' The lady standing in front of the audience asked the question with a smile. She was wearing a bland pink dress. The colour lent brilliance to the hall. There were many people sitting in the hall. The stage was bright. The hall was dark. Although it was completely full, it was hard to see the audience. She stepped forward to the edge of the stage. She was able to see the audience much better now. Not surprisingly, the majority were couples, sitting together. But their faces were expressionless.

No one responded to her. They didn't make any move. Most had tired faces. *Does it matter for us to know the origin of the word?* Their faces seemed to say.

This was what she had expected. Without any hesitation, she answered the question on her own. 'That means "incongruous" in Greek. "Absurd" or "inept" in other words.' Not checking the audience's reaction, she continued her speech, 'The word "atopy" comes from that. So, now, I hope some from the audience here can guess why I'm sharing this information with you.'

She paused and looked around the hall slowly. Her tone went up and her voice got stronger with staccato.

'Atopy is an unclear disease . . . There are no concrete reasons for who gets the illness and who doesn't.'

She took a step back and opened her arms wide, as if she were beckoning someone for a hug.

'So, I want you to know, first of all, that nobody here is guilty.'

Some people seemed to widen their eyes and understand her intention. Still, a few people sat silently.

'That's what I went through as well. I understand all of you. Watching your kids who are crazily scratching their skin till they bleed. They can't sleep because of the itchiness . . . Having inflammation on their skin, they get shy. They are sometimes mocked by their friends. Their friends think they are disgusting.'

She paused and looked at the audience with tears in her eyes.

'Believe me, I went through it. I witnessed the painful experiences my boy went through. He even tried to take some extreme actions . . . on himself.'

She heard some sobbing sounds reverberate in the dark hall.

'When my boy was a kid, I asked the kindergarten teacher to apply some ointment before nap time. She refused but she wouldn't say why. She just said that she wasn't able to do it because she was not used to it. But I was able to see her face, half disgusted and half fearful. Although I told her it was not contagious . . . it was not a disgusting thing. She still treated my boy as a bug.'

More sobbing from the audience.

'What I went through is what you went through, what you are going through. While he was getting older, I had to digest his anger towards me and my husband. In those moments, it all seems like your fault.'

She heaved a big sigh. She had to stop for a moment. There was no noise, not even the drop of a pencil. She shared in a determined voice, 'But as I mentioned in the beginning, no one knows why this is happening to our children. Please don't feel guilty . . . feeling guilty is the biggest source of toxicity we have now.'

She looked around with a steely gaze. She stared at the ladies. 'Mothers! You don't need to blame yourself. I know how it goes, thinking this and that. Wondering if maybe you ate something inappropriate during pregnancy. But that doesn't lead to the torment this disease inflicts.' She turned her attention to the men. 'Fathers! Smoking next to my wife . . . or drinking too much . . . yes, that's bad.' She flashed a slight smile 'But it is still not the reason behind your child's pain.'

The stage seemed to get brighter. Or they brightened the light of the stage. It highlighted the colour of dress and the atmosphere relaxed slightly. 'Unreasonable accusations don't help us at all.' She raised her index finger and placed it next to her mic. 'What we know is but one thing. What many people agree on now is that it is a modern disease. It is an industrial disease. It is a disease that our kids shouldn't suffer from. This is a new phenomenon. We don't know anything about this type of disease. Why is it happening to our children?' She seemed to want to make this the climax, repeating, 'Why?'

She displayed a big and bright smile.

'This is why we are here together. My boy who blamed me and my husband has now completely overcome the disease and I am here to share my experiences. And encourage all of us to share our experiences. That's what this meeting is for. We must remind ourselves that it is not an incurable disease. But first of all, we need to start without guilt. It is not your fault . . . It is not our fault.'

Loa was twelve. He was an adorable son to Sarang and Sangmin. To them, he was smart and considerate. But he was also tortured. Loa was born with atopy. He scratched his body crazily. When it attacked him, his face turned red. He experienced extreme pain. Sarang and Sangmin had to put a pair of mittens on his hands and so he wouldn't hurt his skin. Some people said maybe it was a symptom of moving into a new house.

Many people believed new houses nowadays were built with materials that were not environmentally friendly. That was the main reason for this skin disease. Some people said that the obsessive cleaning habits of those in modern society was the main culprit. 'Kids should play with dirt. They have to be rolling around with sand and nature.' Sangmin's parents sometimes said the same, their voices filled with worry whenever they visited their grandchild in Seoul. However, that was impossible in city life.

'We use so much bleach and disinfectant for sanitation. We bring instant wet towels everywhere we go. Over emphasis on cleaning has brought upon this disaster on modern humans. We never had such a skin disease when we rolled around outside. What grandparents and old generations say is not obsolete. It's the wisdom of the experience.'

Maybe Loa's grandmother was right. Sarang and Sangmin took Loa outdoors to the playgrounds whenever they had the chance. But there was always a limit to how often they went out and how long they stayed. Plus, there was not much sand around. Playgrounds were made of old tires and plastic. There were not many wooden play structures around, not to mention natural materials on the ground. They struggled to find dirt. How ridiculous was that? *We live surrounded by cement*, Sarang and Sangmin realized. They were struck by things that were obvious, but they had not considered before. Living in a big city had been their entire life. Now, as a mother and father, the city looked totally different.

Sarang and Sangmin attended meetings and events related to atopy disease. Some said it was because of food. Too much pesticide and unknown artificial additives. When they learned of this, they only gave organic food to Loa. However, there was not much change. Some said it was due to the lotion they used. Lotions had all kinds of chemicals in them. To help Loa, Sarang even learned how to make lotion and only used home-made lotion on Loa. They did their best. They bought the products that some mothers claimed had cured their kids and followed the advice of the parents who said they'd overcome atopy with their own recipes of food or lotion.

'It is a modern disease. What can we do? Sometimes they get better when they get older.' Some parents consoled them. Sarang and Sangmin were frustrated. *Why only our boy?* Some parents didn't care at all about what they gave to their children, and they were free from this curse.

Sarang and Sangmin took turns to take care of Loa when he woke up in the middle of the night due to the persistent itchiness. When he scratched his body, he scratched till the skin peeled and blood came out. Either Sarang or Sangmin then had to massage his body softly till he fell asleep again.

They were tired, but Loa was their everything. His pain was their pain. *He will get better when we take better care of him.* They also knew many children got better when they got older. *When he gets older, he will be also far better.* They bemoaned their bad days and fervently hoped for better ones.

But what they didn't know was that the worst day was yet to come.

★★★

Loa was sleeping. His itchiness became worse in spring. The dryness perhaps made things worse. Loa's nails had to be cut shorter than usual. He hated getting his nails clipped. But they didn't have a choice. Any length couldn't be accepted.

Spring seemed long this time. Sarang sighed. Every night was a struggle. She had to make sure she was awake till Loa was able to fall asleep. Some days, they were lucky. The night was peaceful. Other days, it was like they were fighting a war. Distracting Loa from the itchiness and putting him to bed was not easy.

When Sangmin was away, it was harder. Tonight, he had to entertain clients who were visiting and take them to dinner. Loa's care was left to Sarang.

Sarang, Sangmin, and Loa usually ended up sleeping in the same room. Usually, one parent gently scrubbed Loa's body while the other distracted Loa from the obsession with scratching.

Loa was perfect tonight. No itchiness, no scratching fever. He fell asleep like a baby. Sarang snuck out of the room. She would go back to bed soon enough. She threw her body on the sofa. Her body was always so tense. Tonight was a lucky night. *Summer must be coming. Maybe I should watch some fun programme,* she thought. Holding the TV remote, she became comfortable on the sofa. Her eyelids grew heavy as she watched her favourite guy with his followers on TV. She even didn't notice when she fell asleep. She was thinking of what she had to do—*I've got to brush teeth. I've got to turn the light off. I've got to go back to Loa*—when sleep claimed her midway.

Suddenly, she heard sobbing. *What is this?* She tried to open her eyes. But it didn't work. She felt shaken. *Am I being squeezed by scissors again*? Memories flashed of being half-asleep and feeling as if she had been pressed violently down. *Wake up*. Her body moved back and forth. The sobbing was as loud as thunder. She forced herself to open her eyes and looked around wildly.

Loa was standing in front of her. Tears streamed down his face. Red tears.

★★★

Loa felt itchy not only on his body, but also on his face, especially his eyes. Sarang and Sangmin were worried about him rubbing his eyes hard. They stopped him, but there was a limit to what they could do. 'At least he is rubbing, not scratching,' the doctor tried to console Sarang and Sangmin.

'He might lose his eyesight. He has only one option—we can transplant both corneas,' the doctor proclaimed.

Atopy affects not only the skin. That's what Loa's parents learned. Sometimes, kids also lose their eyesight. That became their story.

Their efforts were useless. Loa was a complicated case. He had keratoconus and keratitis. He rubbed his eyes or around his eyes because of itchiness. Then his eyelids became inflamed. That impacted his cornea. And he rubbed constantly. His vision was already going. This was how a peaceful night became the worst.

'The cornea is better than other organs. Earlier, people were reluctant to share their own organs or their family members' organs. But the cornea is a little bit different. Of course, people who are stuck in old ideas still say that without your eyesight you or your dead family members can't find the other world and get lost after death. They become ghosts who are wandering around here and there. But the power of superstition has weakened. The age range for cornea donors is much more diverse now. You can look for anyone who is between six and seventy years old. Their corneas can be a fit for Loa.'

The doctor was trying to encourage Loa's parents.

★★★

We were ready for the worst scenario!

Loa was miserable. He couldn't sleep well. All his nerves were focused on the arrival of the monster that would come to him. Loa told Sarang and Sangmin this.

The monster comes to him. It touches him. It is because of the monster's touch that his skin is cursed. When the monster comes, he cries and scratches his skin. He thinks he is cursed. No one around him can share his misery. He always wonders why he was cursed by the monster.

What did I do wrong?

The pain came every day, every moment . . . he gave up on his life. He was such a tiny boy. But he was living in hell.

Then Mini came to him. When he received new corneas, the hospital gave many warnings to Sarang and Sangmin. He could have side effects. It could be trivial. It could be serious. The doctor said that the corneas were ultimately not his. They were alien to him. His body might resist really hard.

Loa's cornea had been damaged severely. The doctor had had to take all three layers of the cornea and use air bubbles on his eyes. When the doctor shoved the small circular blade in his face, Sarang and Sangmin thought he might not be able to make it.

The surgery went well. Then, the miracle came. After the surgery, out of all the side effects that one might experience—dry eyes, expanded blood vessels, eye infection, worse itchiness, self-torture because of the severe pain—none appeared. Loa was at peace. He lay down on the bed without rubbing his eyes. The eye patches were perfectly positioned. The air bubbles were where they were supposed to be. Loa finally found what was right for him. His body finally seemed complete.

Loa later said it was Mini who had conquered the monster.

Chapter 12
Kidney: The Third One

April 2001

'Isn't he a little bit small?'

Again, such an insensitive comment. That hurt Yejin.

Ansoo was growing slowly compared to the same age group. *Yejin and Ahn caught up with other friends later*. That's what they told Ansoo when such comments were thrown at him. Mother-in-law kept nagging Yejin about why Ansoo was not eating well. She thought he was too weak.

'He gags in front of food,' mother-in-law complained. 'Making good food is useless. He is not eating. Or he throws out of his belly.'

Ansoo was a crying baby. He was not an easy boy. That was the cause of a lot of headaches for Yejin and Ahn.

'Some kids grow so fast, we even don't recognize. Some kids make a lot of noise and fuss when they are babies. They are all different human beings. But they all grow anyway. Some kids are difficult, and some kids are easy. Don't worry too much.' When Yejin confessed about her difficulty balancing her work and her responsibility as a mom, this is how her colleagues consoled her.

'Being a working mom is not easy. He might miss you when you are not around. But time passes fast. They soon don't want parents to be around them. You can't give up your career. Be the best mom the moment when you are with him. Quality time is more important. You know I see so many mothers on their phones or busy talking with other mothers while their kids are sitting next to them, desperate for their attention.'

Her colleagues frowned and shook their heads. Yejin nodded firmly, agreeing with their points. *I can be 100 per cent for him when I'm with him.* Yejin tried her best to focus on Ansoo on the weekends. She wanted to sleep late and roll around the bed late morning. Ansoo continually whined about his headaches on the weekend. Yejin tried to entertain him as much as possible.

'He is too weak,' Ahn sometimes complained. 'Kicking a football several times in the park and that's it. He then squats down and doesn't want to do it any more.'

Ahn tried to take Ansoo to his Sunday football club, but he was embarrassed by how weak his son was in front of his club friends. This made Yejin upset, but it was true. Ansoo was not interested in doing any exercise or playing outdoors.

★★★

Yejin had been planning this trip for weeks! Finally, they would have a long vacation. 'Let's drive to the east coast. We can drop by a *matjib*! There will be several matjib on the way driving.'

The rest areas were full of interesting food. Yejin had worked hard to decide the route, even picking which rest areas they would drop by, and which matjibs and cafés they would go to. She'd even skipped lunch at the office, using the time to make her own road trip map instead. *We can visit the rest area for snacks and drop by five restaurants and three cafés!*

She proudly looked at the map, sitting on the passenger seat. Despite their early departure from home, their car had been stuck in Seoul for a while. When they finally managed to drive out of the grey city, they found themselves surrounded by continual layers of mountains.

Leaving the car window of her side open, Yejin wondered why so many people wanted to be stuck in Seoul. *Early retirement would be great*, she thought. She turned her head to check the back seat. Ansoo was asleep. His small body curled up in the backseat. He was still a small baby. His face hadn't change much since his birth. She felt a stab of pain looking at him. He needed mommy. Ahn hadn't liked the idea of a road trip because the club he played for had a Sunday football match, but he had given up the match this time. He'd known Yejin was serious this time. When he'd driven out of the grey city, his face had also brightened and he, too, checked on Ansoo often, constantly glancing at the rearview mirror with a smile.

'Has he done his business?' Yejin asked.

'What do you mean?' Tilting his head, Ahn looked at her.

Drinking sweet coffee after eating beef noodles, Yejin's mouth tasted bitter. *Strange.*

'We drove many hours, and dropped by one café, one restaurant, and one rest area for snacks.'

Yejin's concerned eyes fixed on Ahn. Yejin and Ahn were drinking their coffee next to a small coffee machine. Ansoo crouched down and looked at a dog that was caged at the back of the restaurant. The dog seemed used to being looked at by customers. It didn't care about the boy's presence, not moving in his cage.

'I went to the toilet four times to pee since the trip started. Did he pee when you took him to the men's toilet?'

Ahn scratched his head. 'No, actually he only washed his hands. No pee.' He thought it was weird talking about his nine-year-old son's peeing business. He was not a baby any more. But at the same time, he realized he had relieved himself several times, but not Ansoo . . .

'Did he drink enough liquid?' Ahn asked Yejin.

'Yes. I urged him to drink several times. And we ate soup for lunch . . . He has got to let it out!' Silent, both looked down at Ansoo's crouched back.

'You know . . . kids don't pee as much as we old folks do.'

Yejin squinted at Ahn briefly. 'Let's see. We still have a long way to drive.'

Ahn felt he wanted to pee again. 'Ansoo, no toilet? We are going get back in the car again soon.' He patted Ansoo's head. Ansoo just shook his head, his eyes fixed on the dog.

★★★

'I think we should take him to the hospital.'

After coming back from the road trip, she checked the internet here and there. All his symptoms were linked to kidney dysfunction.

Ahn widened his eyes. 'What? He is only nine. And we don't have any such family history. Bad kidneys are for middle-aged men who have diabetes or high blood pressure.'

'I don't know . . . I think I should take him to the clinic just in case. We wouldn't have known if we hadn't gone on this trip. He doesn't pee. All his other symptoms are connected to kidney dysfunction.'

They finally made it to the doctor. Yejin cried the whole night. Ahn couldn't sleep. He kept going in and out of the apartment.

Acute renal failure.

'Why didn't you come earlier? He must have been suffering a lot. When children get this disease, the symptoms can worsen faster than in adults. Already more than 50 per cent of his kidneys are dysfunctional. What we can do now is kidney dialysis.

But we are not sure how long his kidney can survive. The worst scenario is a transplant. It can take very long time to find a donor. I recommend you apply for the transplant now,' the doctor urged them. The doctor's accusatory tone penetrated Yejin's heart. *I should have quit my job earlier. My greedy desire was killing my boy.*

'The symptoms show gradually. That is what I heard from other doctors. The symptoms are especially hard to detect in children,' Ahn consoled Yejin. It was rare for a nine-year-old boy's kidney to fail. The hospital was perplexed.

★★★

12 July 2001

When Yejin and Ahn had received the call, they couldn't believe it. They had been told it would take the better part of a year—under the best of circumstances. So, they had tried to prepare themselves mentally for a long wait. When the call came just three weeks after the tests, they were almost euphoric. They hurried to the hospital.

Yejin and Ahn didn't have any knowledge about the transplant. Every sentence from the nephrologist was foreign to them.

'You need cold water. That helps to block the blood supply. Taking a kidney from a body is one matter. But how much we can reduce the time between taking out the kidney and transplanting it is key.' The nephrologist continued, 'We will leave his dysfunctional kidneys. We will attach the new one to his body.'

'So will our boy have four kidneys?' Yejin and Ahn were bewildered.

'No, one kidney will be connected to his bladder.'

'Only one?'

'Yes, one kidney transplant,' the nephrologist said simply.

'Does the donor only have one kidney?' Ahn asked.

'No, only one kidney from the donor survived,' she replied.

'Is resorting to one kidney enough?' Ahn continued to question.

The nephrologist peered at them. *Don't be greedy.* Her eyes seemed to say that. Yejin felt embarrassed.

'One kidney will function well as long as your child takes medicine accordingly . . . at least you are lucky. You found a donor in time.' The nephrologist decided not to add, 'Your happiness is possible due to the other family's tragedy.' She felt she should stop now. *Be professional.*

Yejin wondered who the donor was and whether the donor had a healthy kidney. Why had only one kidney survived? But she felt she shouldn't question it further. *The doctor wouldn't share any information about the donor anyway.*

The doctor mechanically added more instructions.

'Keep these instructions in your mind. I will give several more instructions before you sign the letter.' She continued, 'You should let him take the medicine that we give. His life will depend on it. The new kidney needs time to adjust to a new owner. It needs medical help at all times. Promise me that you will be in charge of this. You should ensure your kid follows these instructions.' Both showed their attentiveness eagerly. The doctor's voice was not much different from a robot on the phone at this moment.

'There can be some possibility of changes and risks, such as inflammation, high blood pressure, change in personality. The reason why I am saying this in advance is because you should be aware of the risks of going through with this surgery. Fortunately, he passed all tests, and he doesn't carry the antibody that could attack the donor's organ. But I always make sure the patients are aware of risks before the surgery.'

They continued nodding while typing hurriedly on their phones. All they could think of was how their boy wouldn't have to take steroids, he wouldn't have to take growth hormones, he wouldn't have to undergo peritoneal dialysis. The horrible stories they had read on the internet were not theirs any more.

They were lucky.

Chapter 13
Citron Tea

15 November 2010

'Have you noticed Jihoon's temper?'

Minsu was bewildered and looked at Young.

'What do you mean?'

'I don't know . . .'

Young brought two cups of citron tea and sat in front of Minsu. Minsu wanted to sip the tea immediately but hesitated a little bit. She'd again poured the water when it was too hot. Minsu had told her many times she didn't have to boil the water to a 100 degrees for citron tea. That killed the fragrance. *She must have been distracted,* he thought.

'Jina has gone out with Jihoon several times.'

Young lowered her voice as she shared the big secret. No one was around.

Finally, Minsu was able to catch a whiff of the sweetness and freshness of the citron. Listening to Young, he remembered how Jihoon had talked about Jina several weeks before.

'I thought Jihoon was not interested in going out on a date.' Minsu tried to be diplomatic. 'Don't jump to conclusions yet.'

Young instantly showed some disappointment on her face. 'I know. Jina said they decided to be friends . . . just friends . . .'

As Jihoon had said last time, Minsu thought.

'But I don't know. Jina seems to have a little bit of a different impression of him.' Minsu's gaze was drawn to Young knitted brow.

'What kind of impression?'

'I don't know . . . hm.' Young hesitated.

Minsu took a big sip of tea and chewed on a piece of citron. *Sweet . . .*

Young almost whispered, 'Bad guy?'

Minsu almost choked on the piece of citron. 'But don't women say a bad guy is attractive? Isn't there even a popular term, *nappeun namja*?' He grinned at Young.

'No . . . I mean . . . *literally* bad.' She puffed her cheeks. That meant she was upset about his comment because he hadn't taken her words seriously.

Minsu stuck out his lower lip. At least, it would show he was taking Young's words seriously.

'I'm lost, honey. It's hard to catch up with you.' Minsu wanted to appear thoughtful in response to his wife's concern.

'Jina told me she's not comfortable with Jihoon. She sometimes feels a chill, a cold feeling. Just last weekend, they got together and took a walk along the Han River. And he got a phone call. He picked up the phone hurriedly and walked away fast. She had no idea what to do. So, she followed him. She couldn't hear, but she said he was a completely different man . . . even having a different voice. He was very irritated with the person on the other side, he was not shouting and being mad . . . but he was still really scary. She said he gave her a forbidding look when she tried to check on him.'

Young remembered the look of fear on Jina's face and conveyed it to Minsu.

'Maybe something related to his investment. He can't always be a smiley nice guy.' Minsu tried to defend Jihoon.

Young was quiet and fingered the edge of the cup. 'I don't know . . . Jina said Jihoon looks like a nice guy, but only one layer is nice. Beneath that layer, he seems to have some kind of a bomb. If you touch it, you will set it off and die in the explosion.'

'Who knows? Jina might be afraid that everyone in town will come to know that Jihoon bailed on her. It could be her defence mechanism.' Minsu had known Jina for a while.

'What do you mean?' Young wasn't happy about Minsu's comment and said, 'Don't be so harsh on her, Minsu! I know Jina is noisy sometimes, but she's not that wicked.'

Minsu nodded. He then sighed and said, 'Of course I know she is not. Besides, you know that although the neighbours talk about how nice and gentle Jihoon is, we know he smiles with pain in his heart.'

Young lowered her eyes. 'Yeah, I know . . .'

There was silence. Both drank their tea.

'Did you tell Jina about . . . ?' Minsu broke the silence.

Young shook her head immediately.

'No, no, no. I know Jihoon doesn't want . . . and I also . . . don't want people to know . . . about Gun even though they are our close neighbours. It is a sensitive time for Gun. I don't want him to be distracted by the neighbours' gossip.'

Minsu wanted to make the conversation light.

'Maybe Jina is too sensitive.' Minsu put more citron in the tea. 'Or she is pissed off because he didn't fall for her.' Minsu continued, 'We know Jihoon's history . . . Jihoon can't be always happy and smiley. So, it is understandable why Jina feels strange things from Jihoon.'

'But honey . . . Do you think we really know him? I think we know only one part, not everything,' Young passively protested. 'We don't know him well. We don't know what happened to him and his wife after. We only know one part of his life.'

Minsu hesitated, but he didn't want Young to dive into bigger suspicions about Jihoon. That could be disastrous.

'Jihoon and his wife divorced after what happened to them. They couldn't overcome the trauma together. So that's why he is alone. But he said she is fine and even has a son with her new husband . . . a happy life.'

Young's eyes widened. 'How do you know?' Her accusing glare seemed to penetrate the depths of him.

'He told me,' Minsu said.

'Did he tell you? When? What are you now? Are you his *jeolchin*? When did this happen?' she asked Minsu.

For some reason, Minsu felt proud he was the only one who knew Jihoon's secret. 'I'm just saying he went through a lot. So that's why we should understand him, at least *we* should.'

'I know Jihoon has a heavy tongue. It's surprising you didn't tell me about his wife. I thought I'm your bosom buddy.' Young felt frustrated and excited at the same time. Maybe it was a good thing that Minsu and Jihoon had become Damon and Pythias.

Minsu thought about what Jihoon had offered several weeks before. He hadn't talked about it with Young yet. Minsu had had to hide his smile and excitement the last several weeks.

He had needed help desperately. It was only after that night when he'd met Jihoon and had accepted his offer for a ride that he was finally able to sleep well. His nightmare, which had plagued him for several months, was over. One lucky night had saved him. And the saviour was Jihoon again. To Minsu, Jihoon was a prince on a white horse.

Minsu had not been able to sleep because Young still didn't know how much pension he had pulled out to use on stocks. If he told her about it, then he would also have to talk about how much he'd lost. Minsu was still considering when the best time to talk with Young would be. Jihoon had really turned out to be an angel without wings. Young's suspicion of Jihoon scared Minsu.

Minsu, in his mind, kept telling himself, *I am not defending him because of his offer*. But Minsu also knew he'd already become greedier. *Gun can get some more extra benefits for his future.* In the end, Jihoon was all alone. No wife, no kid.

Minsu suddenly downed his citron tea as if it were a cold beer. Young looked at him. Minsu blushed. Young didn't know what was going through his mind. Minsu wanted to stop this conversation, but Young wasn't done yet.

'I'm glad to hear his wife is happy now. The look on her face, filled with so much pain at that time, sometimes comes back to me.' Heaving a deep sigh, Young continued talking about her suspicions.

'I don't know . . . I like Jihoon . . . because I feel relieved when I see him with my own two eyes. Otherwise, I would have been wondering about Jihoon and Seri my whole life. And I can see Jihoon wants to be friends with us and with Gun. Sometimes, I feel that Jihoon knows more about us than we think. That gives me goosebumps . . .'

Tonight's theme was Jihoon. Minsu sighed. Definitely not a night to talk about Jihoon's offer.

'Why do you think like that?'

'Sometimes, when I run into him, he comments about Gun. He says, "Gun doesn't seem to have many friends. How's Gun? How's his health? How's his school life? Does he sleep enough?"' Young's face showed how upset she was. 'I feel weird. Whenever I try to change topics, it always goes back to Gun. I'm not comfortable.'

Minsu suddenly thought about Jihoon's comment last time. His joy that night had eliminated what Jihoon had told him about Gun. Minsu felt embarrassed. 'Isn't it good? Gun basically has an uncle. I don't have brothers or sisters. Now, Gun basically has a new and very capable uncle who cares about him.' Unconsciously, Minsu's pitch became higher when he said the word 'capable'. Young didn't seem to notice.

She was eager to share more.

'Honey, listen to me. Two months ago, I ran into Jihoon, and he asked me how Gun's math exam outcome for the mid-term was.' Young continued, 'So I casually chatted with him, you know blah blah, because Gun had actually screwed up the math exam. Then Jihoon recommended Teacher Lee to us.'

Minsu was surprised. 'Jihoon was the one who introduced Teacher Lee to us?'

Watching her husband's reaction, Young exclaimed, 'Yes! At that time, even I didn't think much about it. I just thanked him. You know, nowadays, it is hard to find an appropriate tutor, especially with our budget. I just trusted Jihoon. He said Teacher Lee is not expensive, but not bad and has a fair reputation.'

Minsu leaned towards Young, eager to hear more. Young responded to her husband's curiosity. 'As Jihoon said, Teacher Lee demanded an appropriate tuition fee. It was actually rather cheap. I thought maybe that's just his price. Later, I heard from our neighbour Kim, Teacher Lee is a legend in this field. He is a really expensive tutor and famous math tutor. They were shocked when they ran into him at our house and kept asking how we fetched him and how much we pay him. They said having Teacher Lee as a tutor is like catching a star in the sky. People enter their names in the waitlist several years in advance.' Young even gestured as if she was catching something in the air.

'Then, isn't it good for us?' Jihoon was already taking care of Gun's academy! At the same time, Minsu felt jealous. Jihoon was able to do what he, as a father, was not able to do.

Young raised her voice. 'No. Honey, you're not listening to me. Why did Teacher Lee ask for a lower fee from us? I was even scared to ask him directly. But the other day, I saw him enter Jihoon 's house and drive out with his fancy car. He even parked his car at Jihoon 's house. I think Jihoon might be paying him. I mean . . . Teacher Lee seems to receive the rest of the money from Jihoon.'

'Why do you think that? It is too presumptuous.'

'Because he always tells me how generous Jihoon is. Last Friday, I asked him whether they are friends. He said no, he didn't know Jihoon at all. He just got the call from Jihoon for this tuition. When he comes next time, I will ask him directly why he is parking his fancy car at Jihoon's house and whether he gets some money from him. If Jihoon is paying him, I will stop having him teach Gun. The other mothers are burning with jealousy. If they get to know Jihoon is the one behind it, do you know what gossip they are going to spread in the whole community? They will say Gun is actually Jihoon's son!'

Minsu stood up from his chair. Young blushed. She seemed to admit, *I know I went too far.*

Minsu was wondering whether maybe this was, after all, the time he should share Jihoon's offer with Young. Before Minsu started, Young pushed her cup aside and continued, 'I'm a little bit confused about this. Gun did a bang-up job on math for this mid-term! I can't give up on this opportunity. Gun got the best tutor now and he is affordable! But this is not right. I don't know whether I have to directly ask Jihoon about Teacher Lee and compensate him.'

Young can't accept others' kindness. She feels she should compensate him or pay him back . . .

Minsu held Young's hand softly. 'Young . . . I think Jihoon really takes care of Gun. He is maybe really concerned about him.'

'But isn't it a little bit spooky? How did he know Gun's math exam was bad this time? Did you even know? His dad doesn't know, but the neighbour knows and even finds the best tutor in this country to help him. Isn't it strange?'

Minsu blushed. This sounded like a criticism from Young of his indifference as a father.

'Don't forget Jihoon is acquainted with the principal. Maybe the principal talked to him about it.' Minsu, sitting down again, defended himself.

'Gun is not so special that the principal would remember his math exam. And why would Gun be the subject of conversation between them? If that's the case, Jihoon definitely asked the principal about Gun separately?' Young's eyes were full of suspicion.

'Let's not think too much. I am just glad that Jihoon is here, and he became our neighbour.'

Young said, 'I know, I know . . . I am too . . .' She shook her head and continued, 'But I don't know . . . I don't like it. We respect Gun's privacy, but Jihoon seems to know everything about Gun. He even knows which PC room Gun goes to. When he told me, I felt ashamed as a mother. Why do I have to feel such shame? I felt he was criticizing me for letting him go to such a bad place.'

Young didn't stop complaining. 'Going to the PC room is fine, he can use it to take his stress out after studying. But hearing that from a stranger is not pleasant . . . It's a little bit like stalking.' Young thought about Jihoon's question: 'Is Gun up to something?' She shook her head. She tried to wave off her worries. 'Maybe I am overreacting,' she said to the ground.

Minsu patted Young's shoulder and stood up, holding the two cups up. 'I will take care of them. Don't think too much now. We can perhaps talk to Jihoon later.'

Minsu felt he was in the rough. *I need to tell her soon. What shall I say first? That I lost our pension? Or, that we have another gift from Jihoon?*

Minsu put the cups in the sink and turned the water on hard. *Maybe next time . . . next time I can talk about Jihoon's offer.* Minsu also didn't want to defend Jihoon any more. What Jihoon knew about his son didn't make him happy either. It gave him a headache.

He brushed the timing aside. *It might lead to an altercation. Now is not a good time.* He started washing the cups.

Chapter 14
Uncomfortable Reunion

May 2009

'I thought you didn't want to see me any more,' said Jihoon.

Sarang and Sangmin stood awkwardly in the visitor waiting room at the prison. They didn't meet Jihoon's eyes.

'We are really sorry to make you come all the way down here.'

Sarang was holding Sangmin's hand tightly. There was no smile on her face, though she was trying to conjure one. It made the muscles in Sarang's face ache. A lady who couldn't move her face because of poisoned Botox. Her lips were trembling. Sangmin didn't say anything. *He's aged,* Jihoon thought. His wrinkles seemed recent, deep but somehow fresh.

Jihoon felt sad. *They should be happy now. That should be my face.*

'Don't say sorry. Anyway, I had to meet you someday.'

Jihoon had wanted to bring them more lively and positive news. He hoped his statement didn't worry them. They were the ones who didn't want him to be around. The only family who directly, but politely asked Jihoon not to contact them. Then he realized other families could have been on the same page. The old lady had warned Jihoon. Perhaps they wanted to have an entirely new life. That made sense. Jihoon didn't blame them. But Jihoon didn't tell them what he had been preparing for all these kids. First, he had to figure out what was going on here. *Why am I suddenly being summoned?*

'He wanted to talk only to you.'

Jihoon gazed at them. 'Does he remember me?'

They didn't answer Jihoon's question. Sarang lowered her head and started sobbing.

Sarang and Sangmin had been waiting outside. Now, Jihoon walked through a heavy, metal door. Two guards followed him. While Jihoon walked along the chilly, dark corridor, he was able to see the warm and sunny sky through the window. *The irony.*

★★★

April 2009

It had happened so fast.

It was such a nice day. She decided to take her five-year-old toddler and eight-month-old baby on a walk.

'Can you handle everything?' her husband asked her over the phone. His voice was full of concern.

'Why not? We will just enjoy the sun. It is a sunny day. I can't be stuck here.'

She hadn't gone out much after the second one was born. The helping lady said she could take care of the baby at home.

'It's fine. Just help me move stuff to my car. Both should get some good vitamins from the sun,' said the mother. *I need the sun. I want to breathe!* She was desperate for herself.

The Han River was not so far. It took only fifteen minutes to drive there.

'I will park the car near our jogging path. It's close to a convenience store and toilet,' she said, turning back to the phone. She still had to convince her husband.

'Okay, bring a big mat and jackets too. It's still chilly in the late afternoon. I will try to join you guys as soon as I'm off.'

Such a lie! she thought. He hadn't come back home early since the second baby had joined the family. The second one was much harder. The first one had been easy, not crying much. She'd slept well and was always smiling. So, they thought the second one would be the same. Some friends joked that it was a trick. 'When the first one is easy, the second one is the complete opposite!' Yes, they had been right.

She hadn't been able to sleep well for several months. Her husband also didn't come back early. He sometimes came back before they went to bed and hugged the first one tight and played with her. But not the second one. He chose the sofa for sleeping, excusing himself for early work the next day. There wasn't much of a strong attachment to the second one.

'Babies eat, sleep, and poop! Not much I can do to play with him. I will be a fun dad when I'm needed.'

His excuse allowed him to naturally neglect them. *What a selfish excuse!* Taking maternity leave had caused her promotion to be delayed by many years. The decision to have the second one was mutual. She felt betrayed, but it was too late now to turn back.

When this maternity leave ends, I'm going to go totally crazy! Going out and coming back late! She missed the nocturnal city of Seoul. She even missed her whiny boss. Her lack of sleep made her brain feel woozy every day. She had to sleep during the day to be able to function. *But today is a special day. The sun looks so warm. I have spent enough time inside,* she thought. The day care centre was off today—a teacher training day. The energy of the five-year-old could not be exhausted being indoors. It would be better to go out before the downstairs neighbours sent in a complaint.

The sun will tire her out. Who knows? Maybe it will help the baby sleep as well. I have got to get off the twentieth storey! Otherwise, her sombre spirits would go straight down.

It was such a sunny day! Everyone seemed to have come out. There were many kids playing and running around. It was not easy to find an available space for parking. Some people had even brought tents and some sports stuff. *Good!* At least this would keep her daughter busy.

As she was struggling with the two kids and their equipment, a young couple came over and helped her carry her heavy bags. The young man was very kind and carried most of the bags, except the one that was for the baby. Of course, he had the intention of showing off his caretaking abilities to his girlfriend. *Who cares?* She greatly appreciated him and complimented the young woman on the warm heart her boyfriend had. She could see the boyfriend's grin grow after her compliment. He'd got what he had wanted. She'd got the help she had needed.

She settled down and arranged everything. *This is exciting*. She displayed what she had brought. Juice, some snacks, a small table. She'd even brought some paper and coloured pencils.

She laid the baby on the mat. He was not crying. *Wow!* The shade of the trees, the breeze, and sunshine were all a perfect match. Instead of drawing, her daughter instantly took off to a small playground. She was about to stop her, when she thought, *Oh well, everything is visible. Let her play!*

She was able to see her girl from the mat. She had missed this park. Her jogging track near the Han River was busy with people as usual.

Time will pass. I can join them soon. Or maybe I should start jogging from tomorrow. No more laziness. No more excuses.

The sunlight made colours look different to her. Such a small change could bring so much happiness. She thought that maybe it was her anxiety that made the baby cry. She hadn't asked her husband how his work had been. He had just lost a big project. She knew how hard he had worked to get the project, and how disappointed he was. But she still hadn't asked anything. She'd ignored his desperately sad face. *Maybe I should change my attitude. I should be more positive. We are such a lucky family—all healthy and stable. I should stop complaining*. The breeze made her relax.

Living in the middle of the sky is not normal for humans. She hated the apartment. *We should be close to the soil. Maybe it's time to talk about finding a house with a small garden. City life is not fun for kids.*

The daughter was playing well. She played on the slide continually till it tired her out. Her face was full of excitement. It made the mother smile. All will be good. She lay down next to the baby. She watched him. He looked so content. The warm sun, the cozy breeze, and the white noise lulled her to sleep. Her eyelids got heavier.

★★★

Loa grabbed a banana milk from 7-Eleven. A container box had been converted into a convenience store. It was tiny, only one or two customers could get in, choose what they wanted, and get out. But it was always busy with cyclists and walkers. No one complained. All managed to find what they wanted.

He had also got what he wanted. There was no reason to look around the store. Savouring the artificial flavour of banana, he returned to the playground. The sun beat down on his neck. Sitting on a bench, he sipped his drink and looked around. The thick tree leaves cast a shadow over the bench. He was able to cool down. Kids were busy playing. Some parents were standing around awkwardly. Some mothers were busy chatting with their companions and checking their kids. One girl used the slide repeatedly—sliding down then immediately running to stand in line again. Many kids competitively slid and ran back right away in order to not lose their turns. She was competitive. He saw some mothers wrinkle their noses at her.

Where is her mom?

One boy pushed her when she tried to get in the line. She looked scared as she looked around.

'Minho, be careful. Don't hurt yourself.'

Funny. He was the one who pushed the girl. But his mother worried about him, not stopping his behaviour.

The selfish mother returned to her busy conversation with other mothers. The girl used the slide. The boy ran past her again, pushing her in the process. This time, she seemed a little more intimidated and walked away with a puffed mouth. She sat next to him on the bench.

He shot her a few glances. She didn't bother with him at all. Instead, she walked slowly towards the river side. It seemed like she had come here before and therefore knew the path well. He started walking behind her. No one was taking care of her. *What irresponsible parents they are.* He followed her. And he was able to see Mini follow her too. *I chose the right one, then.* His teeth were chattering. *Don't be weird. I have to do it. That's my destiny.*

★★★

There was a high-pitched scream. Some people were busy jerking their heads around, trying to find out where the scream had come from. A few started running towards the scream.

She opened her eyes, startled. She realized she had drifted off to sleep. *How long was I asleep?* The turbulence woke her up. Something had happened. She sat up and looked down at her baby. He was sleeping. His face was well covered by the shadow of leaves.

Her eyes moved to the playground. It was empty. *Where is everyone? Where is my daughter?*

'Call the ambulance!'

'Where are the parents?'

She turned her head towards the noise. She saw the crowd and heard shouts from them. She jumped up from the mat and ran fast towards the noise. The crowd blocked her. But she knew something had happened to her daughter.

★★★

May 2009

A guard opened another door after reaching the end of corridor. Jihoon walked in and then passed through a metal detector. No beeping sound. It didn't matter—the guard came over nonetheless and patted Jihoon down. It was brief. Another guard took him to a small desk and asked him to write his name and put down his signature. There was a blank after 'relationship'. Jihoon hesitated. *What shall I write here?*

'You can write down "friend",' said the guard.

Instead, he scribbled down 'uncle'.

They gestured Jihoon to one of the doors. They didn't follow. When Jihoon stepped inside, they closed the door behind him.

'Finally, I see you again.'

Loa was already there with a guard. Jihoon immediately recognized the radiance of the big smile from the man wearing a blue shirt and pants. Jihoon remembered a small boy. Loa had been the first to be discharged from the hospital. The boy at that time had looked so tired, so restless. He hadn't changed much. He was still small. Jihoon had expected a bigger boy, or man. The change was not striking. That surprised Jihoon more.

Jihoon awkwardly sat in front of Loa. Jihoon wasn't just sad, he was upset too. Loa was handcuffed. His hands were wrapped in thick clothes. *Are the scars on his face a self-inflicted injury? Did he do that to himself? What made him this way?* He looked so grotty. *He shouldn't look like this. He needs to live hard and appreciate his second life!* This wasn't what Jihoon wanted to see. Loa's face had many scratches and scars. Even with his tied hands, he was trying to touch his neck and body. He was struggling. He looked like he was in pain.

'You remember me.' Jihoon smiled at him. *Did his parents talk to him about me?*

Loa's eyes were restless. He suddenly jumped over and tried to get his face closer to Jihoon's over the table.

A guard shouted, 'Keep to yourself!' Loa backed out of Jihoon's face and sat back down.

Jihoon, trying to stay calm, responded, 'So, your parents said you were looking for me. That is surprising. I thought they hadn't talked to you about me.'

Loa was not interested in what Jihoon had to say. He lowered his voice, trying to whisper. 'You know . . . she wasn't dead.'

Jihoon frowned. He tried to read the meaning behind Loa's words.

'She always followed me. She was standing here and there. She didn't talk, but I was able to see who she was.'

'What are you talking about?' Jihoon tried to concentrate on Loa. But somehow what Loa said distracted him . . . shaking him deeply.

Loa could hear an edge in Jihoon's voice. His face now wore a look of excitement. Finally, he could share his secret.

'I'm not crazy. I'm not hallucinating. I'm talking about Mini.'

His eyes were full of anticipation, relieved that he could finally disclose this secret.

'She didn't die. That's why I'm cursed.'

Jihoon's head was shaken up by the enormity of what this boy was saying.

'What did you just say?'

'They took hers and put hers into me and others. She begged them to stop. She screamed and cried. No one listened. She was shattered . . . shattered . . . looking for her dad. Looking for her mom.'

Loa continued, 'I told Mom. I told Dad. About everything. About Mini. But they didn't believe me. I had to console her on my own. I had to make her pain peaceful. Then I found the girl on the playground. Mini liked her. She chose her. Her mother didn't care. She was just sleeping while her daughter was being bullied. The girl was lonely. Mini needed the company. She needed company too. That's why I did it. I did it for your daughter. She told me that's how I could be freed from this curse.'

Jihoon was watching him. *What do you mean? She wasn't dead?* Loa's words pierced Jihoon's heart sharply. At the same time, Jihoon's brain was working overtime. But his lips couldn't move. He tried to jog his memory, back to the day he'd heard from the doctor that Mini was dead. *I did ask so many times. Wait! What did they exactly say? Do I remember?*

'We are all cursed. We have to save ourselves. I tried to wriggle out of this nightmare, but I failed . . . I couldn't satisfy Mini because the girl survived. Mini couldn't take her. My itchiness will kill me. I will be shattered like her.'

Loa jumped out of his chair. He started twisting his body crazily. He rolled around, trying to rub his body against any available surface. His itchiness came back. He started wailing. 'My skin stinks. I can't stand it any more. You should help me and Mini. You're my last hope.' He begged Jihoon, his eyes full of tears, 'We have to help her soul. Find a way!'

The guards rushed in and tried to take Loa away from the room. And the last words Loa said to Jihoon, Jihoon wouldn't forget. 'I saw the last scene Mini saw, a car running towards her, fast, and her last image with these eyes was of you, holding the phone . . . that last scene keeps coming back to me and then melting before my eyes.'

Jihoon was sitting there alone. He could feel the wrinkles in his brain expand and shrink.

Chapter 15

Liver: Yellow Baby

May 2001

Bian Trinh didn't like it when they mixed dialects. They seemed to do it intentionally and talked about her secretly. But she had to put up with it. Han said they would move out soon. But they hadn't, not yet. It was the third year since she had moved here.

She'd liked Han immediately upon seeing him in Vietnam. Compared to her other friends' husbands, he was not old. He had a genuine smile and a beefy face. Bian Trinh's parents liked it. It meant that he had been nurtured with good food. He even tried to speak some Vietnamese with her parents and sister.

'My study is not good enough.'

He also had a regular job, working as a government officer.

'I'm not a high level. Just ninth.' He showed nine fingers when he talked about his job. She heard his house was not in Seoul. 'It takes only two to three hours by train. Seoul is really close.'

Bian Trinh learnt that you could go to Seoul from anywhere in Korea within five hours with a fast train. But she didn't mind. She was not interested in living in a big city. She didn't like any pretty looking Korean boys in dramas. Her friends all had their own husbands in their wallets. Such pretty boys, their imaginary husbands that never came true. She didn't mind that Han had been married before. She didn't care Han didn't look like the boys on television.

'Let him drink as much as possible. Then you will see what kind of guy he is.'

That's what her parents did the first night when he visited their house.

'Give him high degree alcohol. Let's see how he acts then.'

Han didn't refuse the offer. He took everything when her parents and relatives gave shots. He just fell asleep. He said he couldn't drink much. Maybe he was right. He snored loudly through the night. The parents were relieved. They had heard many bad stories before. 'He didn't seem like a bad guy.' Bian's sister said.

Han's town was quiet. Bian encountered other girls from Vietnam. They didn't like the town. They were eager to move to Seoul. Some regretted their long journey. Some had terrible homesickness. Bian was a positive lady. Han was nice to her. But he was rather reticent. He didn't talk much. He smiled. Rather than talk, he smiled. He came back home on time. The hobby they shared was badminton. When Bian was stressed out by her mother-in-law, Han took her out to the town gym. They played badminton in the indoor stadium. She fell in love with the stadium. It was near the river. Many town people came out and played sports in front of the river or they used this indoor stadium. It was the fanciest place in town.

'This town seems to have a lot of money,' Bian joked to Han. Han smiled. That was Han's job. Taking care of the town. He said his daily job was very monotonous. Every day was the same. But at least it was stable.

One problem Bian had with him was having to live with Han's parents. Bian didn't mind it in the beginning. A big family was what she was used to. But then she got to know why Han's previous wife had left. Her mother-in-law was famous in the town. A noisy big mouth. She talked incessantly. She never stopped. She yelled. She said she just talked. But she yelled. That gave Bian a headache.

She had needles on her tongue. In the beginning Bian couldn't understand a single word her mother-in-law spoke. The accent was too strong. Bian studied Korean hard. Her effort brought a good outcome. Except with her mother-in-law. She was on a different level. Her language seemed to be from nowhere. Bian sensed her mother-in-law enjoyed her perplexed face. Other people tried to talk slowly. They worked hard not to use dialect with her. But not her mother-in-law.

Bian strove to study the dialect too. She gradually began to understand what her mother-in-law was saying and understood why some people said she had needles on her tongue. Especially after Bian gave birth.

Everyone was happy because she'd been able to birth the baby that Han's first wife couldn't produce. A boy. They named him Nomin. Han's mother was happy. But she kept telling Han, 'Why is the baby so yellow? Even his eyeballs are yellow.'

Whenever she saw her grandson, she said, 'Maybe because he is not pure . . .'

Bian was very upset. But she didn't argue back. Han just chuckled. 'Mom is an old-fashioned lady. You don't know how much she likes you.' Bian felt inclined to blurt out that the old lady should see her own skin. Maybe the baby got the skin colour from the old lady.

The baby's skin was yellow. That was true. Bian also thought so. Bian called her mother and talked about it. Her mother said, 'Breast feeding sometimes makes the baby's skin yellow. Don't worry. That's a common thing for breast-fed babies. You also had it. It will go away. What's wrong with yellow skin? He is just a baby. He will be fine.' Bian's parents were concerned but tried to console their daughter.

Their kind neighbour also said, 'Don't worry. The baby's liver takes time to function. Maybe his liver needs more time.'

'Your milk is not enough. Let him get used to it. Breastfeed him as much as possible.'

He seemed to get better. Bian started producing more milk. He was growing well. Except for the white poop sometimes.

'He's not yellow . . . he is just dark.'

The mother-in-law brought her friends and showed the baby to them. They surrounded him and made all kinds of judgements.

'He is like his mom. She has sallow skin.'

Endless speculation. Endless judgement.

Bian didn't like it. Immediately, they would lift their eyes to Bian and examine her.

She felt sick.

'Old people are rude . . . please understand them. It will go away.' Han held Bian's hand softly.

Nomin passed his 100-day celebration. Bian was exhausted. She had had to make white rice bread. Each bread with a pretty package was marked with the number 100.

His skin had turned yellower. His belly had stiffened. His breathing had become rough. One night, instead of white or yellow poop, Bian saw black. She woke Han up and demanded to go to the clinic right away.

Something was not right.

The doctor said something. Bian's Korean was much better now. But all medical words sounded foreign. The doctor's face was solemn. She didn't know what to do, just standing next to them. One middle-aged woman walked over to them and stood there.

'They are saying your baby is diagnosed with biliary atresia.'

The lady spoke in Vietnamese to Bian. Bian grabbed her arm. 'Do you know what they are saying?'

'I have been here for a while.' The lady had instantly known Bian was a Vietnamese wife. The lady held Bian's hand warmly and patted her. Bian almost said, 'Help me, Mom.' Han and the doctor ignored them and continued their conversation.

'Why didn't you take the baby to the hospital earlier? It seems that he must have shown some symptoms.'

Biliary atresia?

'That's like . . . the biliary tract was blocked . . . so the liver cannot function . . . basically his liver is not functioning.' She pulled Bian further away from Han and the doctor so they wouldn't be distracted. She told the doctor in Korean quickly, 'I will fill her in about your conversation.' The doctor nodded briefly.

'Didn't the baby have symptoms . . . like yellow skin?'

Bian almost fell to the ground.

'I thought that was just jaundice from breast feeding.'

'I don't know, maybe . . . according to the doctor, most babies show serious symptoms, yellow skin or black or bloody poop... But some babies display symptoms later. Several months later.'

Bian held the old lady's arms tightly with her hands. 'What shall we do? What's going to happen?'

'Your husband will explain in detail later . . . but you should have brought him in earlier to check it out.' She avoided Bian's eyes and walked away. She called back, 'I'll be back to check on you. Sit on the sofa. Wait for your husband.' *She needs a little time to digest*, she thought.

Bian later learnt that the baby's liver was already not functioning, and he would have to go through surgery. He needed a new liver.

Chapter 16
Decision

11 July 2001

'Mini is brain dead,' said Dr Lee.

Seri turned pale and leaned her entire body against the wall. She mumbled to herself, 'Brain dead.' She seemed to know what that meant. Jihoon looked at Seri and stepped forward towards the doctor. Jihoon was desperate.

'That means we have some hope. I see in the news that they wake up sometimes. We can wait, no matter how long it takes.'

He tried to squeeze his brain to think about any possibility.

Dr Lee seemed accustomed to this situation. Her voice was stable.

'Those cases are different. They are not brain dead.'

'Isn't that the same thing?' *How much medical knowledge do I have?* Jihoon tried to challenge her. He turned to Seri. She had studied biology. Didn't that help now? But she was in a different place already. Her eyes were empty, and she seemed like she didn't want to have eye contact with Jihoon.

Dr Lee spoke slowly. 'When someone is comatose, that person's brain still functions. They are different situations. Although someone in a coma has poor functions in the cerebrum and cerebellum, the brain stem remains active. They can still breathe on their own. So, that's why sometimes, but very rarely, people in a coma wake up.'

Dr Lee continued, 'Brain dead people cannot recover. There is a zero per cent possibility. The whole functioning of the brain has ceased.'

The doctor said all of this without breathing, in a monotonous tone. *I hate this voice*, she thought to herself. It was heart wrenching. She wanted to be done with this moment. More questions, and more answers made her miserable too.

'How are you so sure her brain is completely dead? We have been waiting for her to wake her up. Please do something . . . It might just look like her brain is dead.' Jihoon's tone rose in his desperation. For six weeks, they had had hope. Tiny and desperate but still hope. They had waited for her to open her eyes and smile at them again. The possibility had existed.

Dr Lee had heard about the accident. She had heard about who had been there at that moment. The small girl she had examined thoroughly already looked so peaceful, but the same could not be said about her dad. Maybe he will never be at peace. They had run every kind of test. Dr Lee wanted a miracle as much as the parents did. *The dad will not give up. Of course, he can't give up till he realizes there is no possibility here. I have to be calm, not giving the slightest hope. That's for people who are left behind.* Dr Lee lifted her glasses up from her nose.

'We go through two steps carefully before we announce this. We check her pupillary reflex. We also check the corneal reflex. No reaction. We also go through vestibulocochlear reflex. That means we put cold water in her ears and check whether there is some response in her eyeballs. There was no response. We take a respiratory test and check whether she can breathe on her own.'

Dr Lee explained everything slowly in detail. She had to. She felt the pain in her heart. She had a daughter of similar age. *Life is harsh.* Explaining in detail was all she could do at this moment. The girl's parents had never left the hospital and had witnessed every test. They knew the entire medical story. It was time for Dr Lee to be determined and pronounce the final answer.

'Six hours later, we go through the same process. In Mini's case, the outcome of both those processes was the same.' Dr Lee decided not to look at Jihoon's face while she waited for his response. Silence.

She immediately continued, 'Then we go through the second process. We have the brain-dead assessment committee. We go through the process together and there should be unanimity before we make a final and certain decision about the patient's condition.' She made sure not to forget any small details.

'We try our best till we go through this process.' The doctor knew this sounded like an excuse. But the hospital also knew that it had to show a determined face at this moment. Otherwise, it might bring some doubt or frustration to the family. Then they wouldn't want to acknowledge the death. As a mother, the doctor fully understood them. But she had to act as a medical professional. There could be no confusion, no ambiguity that was shown to them.

'I am really sorry to convey this news,' she added.

A long, weighty silence. The families always reacted in extremes, either wailing and crying, lamenting right after the news, or deadly silence. They couldn't digest the outcome.

The reaction of the girl's parents was that of the latter extreme. Both were silent. That made it hard for the doctors. If at least one member broke down, then the others would focus on that family member. Then the doctors could excuse themselves. But when all were still staring at the doctor with no response to the statement, that was very hard . . . they didn't know what to do. Or they still denied what was happening. Then they would ask the same question. The doctor would have to repeat the answer. But reading their faces, Dr Lee knew they understood what she had said. She was rather relieved.

It was time for the doctor to exit the stage and the administrator to turn up. Then it would be time to talk about the next possible stage.

'Please find me when you need more explanation . . . I am truly sorry . . . We really did . . . our best.'

Her voice got smaller and smaller. Dr Lee looked around. Mr See was standing there. *It is your turn.*

Making eye contact with Mr See, she awkwardly walked away. She tried not to make any noise. When she turned the corner, she sped up, walking back to her office as quickly as possible.

Mr See knew this was the most difficult job. Only thirty-six out of a million brain-dead people donated their organs. The decision was mostly up to the family since the majority did not expect to die in such conditions. He had to do his job well and try persuading the family. 'I am sorry that you just lost your family member. But would you mind giving the deceased's organs to other people?'

He was sometimes pushed . . . and someone had once spat in his face. Many lost it when they heard from Mr See. He heard all kinds of swearing from family members. But he knew this was his job. He knew it could save many people. He walked towards them. If family members cried, he waited. He sometimes held their hands. They did not know who he was, but they needed anyone who could share their tragedy. They appreciated it. Mr See checked the deceased's age, health, and their status at the moment of their death. Then he would count one, two, three . . . Her case could be five. Her intestines were damaged. The marrow would also be out. She was too young. One kidney was recovered from the accident. Then, the lungs, a set of corneas, heart, and liver. He did not like his job, counting the possibilities, but on the other hand, he could see people being reborn. That motivated him. He could put up with being spat on, being pushed, sometimes even punched. He could do it even knowing that the surgeons received all the gratitude in the end. He was a shadow.

Mr See walked towards Jihoon and Seri.

Chapter 17
Resurrection

12 July 2001

Sunday morning, they all received calls from the hospital coordinator, Mr See.

'Please come to the hospital prepared. We might have found a donor.'

The parents immediately rushed to the hospital and as they had already received detailed instructions, they were more than ready.

'Who is the donor?'

The question was not important. Whether their kids would pass the test and could be recipients was.

They all prayed to their own gods.

'Don't have high hopes yet.' That was the unanimous comment parents heard from their own doctors.

'Your kid is very lucky.'

They were flooded with joy and the sense of a miracle.

Mr See printed out the compiled documents regarding the recipients. The cover page was a simple list. A list of the winners. Just a few won this lottery. He went over the list, just once more, following the names deliberately with his index finger.

Ansoo for the kidney.

Nomin for the liver.

Gun for the heart.

Eunwoo for the lungs.

Loa for the new corneas.

Satisfied that the list was accurate, Mr See then prepared a signature form—a golden ticket—for the families of each of the recipients and then one for the donor's family. Sliding the forms into six yellow envelopes, he headed towards the operating area.

★★★

Loa went through a basic set of tests. Compared to other operations, a cornea transplant was rather simple, but that did not mean that you should take it lightly. The corneas would still be alien to Loa's body. His body could reject them.

What happened then? In a short time after the transplant, if Loa's body did not like the new visitors, his eyesight would dramatically worsen. Or his eyes might get congestive. Or he may have eye sores.

Loa's parents were nervous.

'But listen,' they were told. 'As long as we can catch them in early stages, we can take immediate action, such as simple surgery to lessen those adverse reactions.'

Those adverse reactions were not abnormal. He might have small reactions in one to three years. As long as he got along with his new friends, well, then everything would be fine. From now on, his parents should teach him well. Don't rub the eyes harshly even if they are itchy. Eyes are sensitive.

Loa's parents nodded firmly. Sarang bit her lip to stop herself from crying. *It is a good day. It is a good day.*

'Then, I will see you after the surgery.' The doctor walked away.

Later on, the parents were able to learn the donor's parents made one determined condition. Patients under the age of fifteen were to be given priority. A similar age match would mean a lower chance of adverse reactions. Of course, the hospitals happily agreed.

When Mr See told them they could meet the donor's parents if they wanted, the families all agreed. He added that they did not have to. Donor parents and recipient parents' information are officially classed as confidential. How much information is exposed to the other is for the families to decide. If the recipients didn't want to meet the donor, their identity would be kept a secret.

When the recipients said, yes, they would like to meet the donor, Mr See explained who the donor was, and what had happened to the donor. He also shared her photo with them. Recipients' parents knew roughly how old the donor was and what had happened to her. When they saw her photo, they couldn't help feeling both—joy that their own children had been granted a second chance, and grief for the young girl—at the same time. She was an angel to them. And she looked like an angel when they saw the photo.

Chapter 18
Secret

February 2014

Jihoon was not the only one on a nocturnal promenade. A girl was crying.

He instinctively hid himself behind a tree. *What am I watching?*

Gun was there, too. The girl cried and Gun looked down at her as she kneeled down. She was grabbing Gun's pants. In lazy gesture, Gun pushed her away from his leg and slowly trod her down with his leg. Her body was pushed down to the ground. It looked rather like a stage. *Are they acting in the middle of night?*

Jihoon turned pale. He was hesitating about whether he needed to run to the playground. No one was around. It was 2 a.m. It was as dark as it could be. And that side was covered by a big tree. What

Jihoon could see clearly was Gun's serious face reflected by the moon. He was wearing a long black coat. Jihoon couldn't see the girl's face. Her hair was noticeably orange. He felt a clammy atmosphere on the playground.

Gun didn't hit her and didn't push her further. She didn't scream either. Gun stared at her as she cried for a moment. Then, he pulled her body up, grabbing her arms. Gun moved his face close to her. The movements were smooth. Like he was doing *t'ai chi* under the moon. She didn't look at him, continuing to whimper. Gun was telling her something. Jihoon strained his ears but couldn't hear. He was only able to see Gun's face. Gun smiled at her and said something. But his smile made Jihoon uncomfortable. It was a face that Jihoon had not seen Gun make before. It was a face Jihoon would never forget. The girl started crying harder. In contrast to her crying, Gun's face was now full of pleasure. And when Gun released her, she squatted down. Jihoon could hear her choke on a sob. In the darkness and silence, her choked sobs warmed the cold air.

Gun sauntered away. He didn't know Jihoon was watching. Gun whistled pleasantly. It was a chilly night. Gun crossed his arms across his chest so he could trap warmth. He had been perplexed when he'd got to know that she'd come to see him. That was a big mistake. *How brave she was! How did she dare to appear in front of me?* It shouldn't have happened and it wouldn't happen again. He thought she would be strong and could be a good cover. Gun chuckled. *She is a cute slave. I need to give her more homework.* He snuck back into his house.

Jihoon stood stock still for a while. The girl hunkered down and cried. The half-light from the playground lamp was protecting her. Jihoon slowly approached the girl.

★★★

'Gun doesn't have many friends.'

Yoon was drinking a beer. He seemed hungry and thirsty. He was glad to have fried chicken. So glad he hadn't even thanked Jihoon for the beer and chicken.

This, Jihoon already knew. Gun did not seem interested in having many friends.

'Why not?'

'He is not the kind you can chum with.'

'Have you contacted him recently?'

'No way. He doesn't contact me. He's always too busy.'

'Why is he so busy?'

'His computer and phones are his best friends.'

'Aren't you all like that?' Jihoon said sarcastically. Yoon stopped eating. Jihoon picked up a chicken wing and gave it to Yoon with a smile.

'No. He's on a completely different level. Gun is quick with this stuff, internet hacking and coding. The boy is really good! I have sincere respect for his ability.' Yoon bit some flesh off the chicken. He seemed satisfied. 'Maybe that's why he always berated us . . . such a cocky attitude. He was so cold.'

'Are you snooping around trying to find stuff about Gun by talking to his friends?' Yoon narrowed his gaze. He slathered the sauce on the chicken wing. *That doesn't look healthy*, Jihoon thought. 'You know what? You were our favourite topic of gossip for a while, back in high school.' Yoon finished the rest of the wing and drank the beer. Jihoon ordered another bottle of beer. He smiled. 'I know. How did the rumours end?'

'Oh well, we knew you were the principal's friend and tried to help out. And a rich guy who is a close friend of Gun . . . and a godfather who financially supports him. Gun is such a lucky jerk. We were just jealous. We made jokes to provoke Gun. His response was more fun. That's why we harassed him. Besides reacting to rumours about you, he never showed any reaction. He is a stone.'

'Stone?' Jihoon was curious and he saw Yoon was in a talkative mood.

'Gun is rather indifferent. We liked him. He looks . . . hmm.' Yoon put the beer on the table. 'He doesn't care about small matters. He's cool about everything. We knew he had some medical condition. The PE teacher tried not to push him. But Gun completely ignored the PE teacher's concern. He was a good basketball player. You know . . . he was, like, beyond our age.'

Yoon lifted his shoulder up and down lightly. Jihoon could feel that Yoon really wanted to be close to Gun. 'But Gun was very indifferent. He didn't care. So, he was a guy we didn't take lightly.'

Yoon flashed a sly smile. 'Only one thing . . . when I made fun of him and you, he got very upset.'

That hurt Jihoon. 'Did you find some odd things about him?' Jihoon knew his question was weird. 'Gun's parents are worried about him. You know I'm his godfather. They are worried about him. Gun doesn't have to go to military service due to his medical condition, but he seems to insist,' Jihoon lied.

'His parents are concerned about why he has suddenly changed his mind.' Jihoon hoped that Yoon wouldn't contact Gun after this meeting. He was relieved after talking more with Yoon. They were not really close to each other. At the same time, Jihoon was frustrated to know Gun didn't share anything with the people around him.

'Ha ha, can I swap with him? Or he can go to military service instead of me.'

Yoon shook his head. 'I don't know him well either. I never felt that I was close to him, although I tried.' He continued, 'But there's one thing I have always felt was strange . . . you know we use our phones or computers a lot for games. And Gun also used them a lot. But he was not interested in playing games. He always said that those games are not exciting enough. We were busy making our game avatars and buying weapons for them, but he never did any of that. He also always went to PC rooms solo. He never went to the PC room with us. Always alone . . . He has too many secrets. He doesn't share anything with his friends.'

Yoon had almost finished the whole fried chicken.

Jihoon thanked Yoon. He walked back home. He shuddered with unease. *How many are involved?* Gun hid himself completely and perfectly. Jihoon clenched his fists. He could feel his heart pumping fast.

Chapter 19
A New Pattern

2014–2015

'I didn't want to do that.'

Policeman Kang had heard these words from a young teacher he had interrogated. Usually, the criminals would deny what they did. Strongly with anger or with tears. The usual excuse at first was, 'I didn't do that,' not, 'I didn't want to do that.' This woman had been different. She had enticed her eight-year-old students to do shocking things. She had even received awards as teacher of the year several times. Parents had loved her.

Sitting with her in the cell room, Kang remembered feeling odd. She had not seemed like the type to have such guts. She had been completely withdrawn. *Is she disingenuous?* He had tried not to lose his cool, but had shouted at her, 'Then why did you do that?' Her continual denial had begun upsetting him.

She had sobbed hard and seemed to want to say something. But instead, she had laid her head upon her arms and continually cried.

'Don't evade.' Kang had scowled into the fire. 'What were you trying to do with it? Are you saying someone set you up? You did it. You were the one who forced them to do it and recorded it.'

Such a young teacher. What she had done to her students had been disclosed soon after. The victim had not been the only one targeted. The school had also gotten embroiled in the crime. *Didn't she know that would happen?* She had been sent back home first. When the police station had called her in for the investigation again, Kang had been told that they had found her body in her closet.

★★★

'I didn't want to do that.' The same sentence, months later. But this time it was a girl with orange hair who was sitting in front of Kang. *A strange new pattern*, Policeman Kang thought. *Is this the third time?*

Her statement reminded Kang of the teacher. She and her accomplices—a sixteen-year-old boy and a seventeen-year-old boy—had said exactly same thing. *They didn't want to.* This orange-haired girl was the same. She was the main leader of a bunch of teenage girls. They had forced their friend to engage in prostitution. The police had separated all of them and were investigating each. They had all blamed the main leader—the orange-haired girl. She had been called in front of Kang, but she hadn't made eye contact with him at all. Her face looked both guilty and indifferent. She reminded him of the teacher Kang couldn't save and couldn't punish.

'Why did you do that?' Kang patiently asked her.

She kept saying she didn't want to. She kept repeating that the other friends were involved because of her. So, she should be the one who should get punished. *What a hero!* Kang almost spat. He wondered whether she knew all other girls had already pinned it all on her. *Or did she give such an order to them?*

'If you didn't want to, you didn't have to.' Kang tried to get some answers. There might be some accomplice or a real leader behind all these girls.

'Did someone threaten you?'

'I have nothing to spill.'

When Kang had asked the question, he was sure that he'd seen some tears in her eyes.

He waited. He gave a little bit more time to her. *Perhaps she was intimidated and that's why she did such horrible things. What kinds of threats were they?* He thought about the video he had seen. Feeling ill at ease, he walked out of the investigation room. *Maybe I need another tactic.*

After a while, he re-entered the room, with two packs of banana milk and red bean bread. 'Are you hungry?' He pushed a pack to her. She didn't touch it. 'I didn't have breakfast or lunch. You know we are busy nowadays. When the school is on vacation, we police become busier.'

She didn't have anyone to show up to be with her. She was there alone for several hours. The situation was all too familiar. Kang sighed. Her parents knew they should be there together with her. The police went through their procedures, writing down personal information. Her parents were contacted immediately. Both made an excuse that the other side would come first, but no news came from either side. She seemed to be used to this situation and said that she didn't need any guardian.

Kang split the red bean bread in half and put one piece in his mouth. 'I'm partial to red bean bread. Nowadays, it is hard to find the bread made with domestically grown red bean. The red bean has become too sweet now. It went well with banana milk before. But now, I feel that also is too sweet. Maybe I should switch to plain milk.' Kang finished the bread. She still hadn't touched her portion. But at least she was eyeing the packet carefully.

Kang tried to set off the conversation again, but a little differently this time. 'Have you heard about gaslighting?'

Kang didn't look at her. He started narrating a story as if there was no audience in front.

'There was a boy, seventeen. He got to know a woman who was older and was a practice teacher. She came to his school as a practice teacher, along with several other practice teachers. He liked her. You know teenage boys can have a crush on an attractive teacher. Earlier, he had not been interested in studying. But maybe she gave him the motivation he needed. He started studying. Love changed him. The practice teacher also gave some private tuition to him. His grades got better. Nice story so far.'

Kang took a big sip from the straw, and continued, 'A month after the teaching practice, she left the school and went back to her hometown. He was sad. They still contacted each other. The practice teacher suggested to his parents that they send him to her hometown during the summer break. The parents were surprised by her offer. She told them she could find a small dorm for him and privately tutor him since the university entrance exam was coming soon.'

The orange-haired girl gazed up at Kang. She looked puzzled by the sudden story and showed curiosity about the story at the same time.

Kang continued, 'What do you think the parents did? Of course they approved. The boy was too sad. And he couldn't focus on studying. After she'd left, his grades had become worse than before. I don't know if the parents knew about this small crush he had. Maybe if they'd known, they would have made a different decision.' Kang paused briefly but went on. 'So, the parents handed their son some money and let the practice teacher take care of him till the exam. She was a saviour to the parents. *An angel without wings*, they thought. But she made the parents agree to a condition. Don't visit him! So, he can really focus on his studies.'

Her eyes fixed on Kang with puzzlement. Now, they finally made eye contact. It encouraged Kang to continue the story.

'That's odd, right? But the parents believed her. Her words seemed to ring true. She was from a very good university. Her honesty . . . they assumed she was nice, a person with integrity. Or they were desperate—as all parents are when their kids' big exam comes up. They tried to contact him several times, but only messages were allowed. He said everything was good . . . the exam date was coming. They tried to contact him, but no phone call. Only messages. "I'm doing fine. I'm studying hard." Everything was very brief. They felt that something was odd. So, they broke the rule she'd made. They drove down to the town and looked for him. They finally went round to find the location they could see from the phone. They found him dead in a house, the house where the practice teacher's friend lived. Their son had been beaten to death. Not just once. He was consistently tortured and sexually abused. A boy of seventeen. An energetic age but still vulnerable.' Kang paused a little, but he didn't feel like drinking his banana milk. 'What they saw was hell.'

He added instantly, 'We arrested the house owner and her boyfriend immediately. She admitted she did kill him with her boyfriend. They let him stay at her house and then they tortured him.'

The orange-haired girl pursed her lips. Kang saw anxiety in her eyes. Kang paused for a while and stared at her.

'Do you think the teacher's friends did it?' When Kang asked her, she didn't respond, but he could feel that she was eager to hear the next chapter.

'We also had the same thought at first.' Kang shook his head. 'The girlfriend . . . yes . . . she committed murder with her boyfriend. Very cruelly. They didn't have any criminal record at all. A very ordinary young couple. But she did it because the practice teacher had ordered her to.' Kang collected crumbs of the bread from the desk. 'It is hard to believe. They were friends for a long time . . . since secondary school. They were best friends. The practice teacher was very nice. When her friend went through economic hardship, she helped her and listened to her problems. That's how they bonded and shared everything with each other . . . at least the practice teacher's friend shared everything. But even she didn't know what kind of person the practice teacher was. The practice teacher completely disguised herself and manipulated her friend. That's what we call gaslighting. Humans can be completely dominated and manipulated by others. But many don't recognize it till the end.' Kang sighed unconsciously. 'It was so cruel. How the boy was tortured. You can't imagine how cruel humans can be; how much we still don't know about humans.

One saw friendship in their relations. The other saw a game.'

There was a silence. The orange-haired girl didn't say anything, but her shock and fear was delivered through the air to Kang. Kang continued, 'I asked the manipulator why she did it . . . manipulating her best friend who she had helped for a long time, ordering her to kill an innocent boy who thought he was in love . . .'

'What did she say?' Finally, the orange-haired girl, flinching, interjected with a question.

Kang frowned as he thought about the moment. 'She said she just did it for fun. She wanted to know how far her friend would go for her . . . so, she said she tested it . . . The innocent boy was desperate to be close to her and the money from his parents was good. But she got bored, so she wanted to have fun. And that's the way she had fun, destroying two people's lives.'

The orange girl's face showed her disbelief.

'The story doesn't make sense, I know.' Kang sighed. 'Can there be a devil? If you ask me, yes, I would say, yes, absolutely. There are monsters out there wearing human masks and living with us.' Kang clasped his hands together. 'And it's getting more and more difficult to catch those guys nowadays because they've gotten smarter. They are so good at disguising themselves now.'

Kang looked at the orange-haired girl and asked slowly, but clearly, 'Are you a victim of gaslighting?'

Kang strongly believed that she was not the main one. Kang could feel it. Something was happening. She perhaps didn't recognize she was manipulated by other humans. Friendship or love . . . it could have been disguised under names from a beautiful vocabulary.

The orange-haired girl showed her entire face to Kang. No more avoiding eye contact, no more lowering her head. But she was not watching Kang. She was watching something else. She was somewhere else. Her eyes were full of fear and anxiety. Kang could tell. She opened her mouth. Her voice sounded strange, muffled.

'What?' from Kang.

She looked at Kang but suddenly pursed her lips. She lapsed into silence. She avoided eye contact and became as she had been.

Someone knocked on the door and opened it. 'Her grandmother is here.'

They were threatened. That's what Kang concluded. However, all Kang could do at the moment was watch her walk away with her grandmother. Her crimes were obvious. There was evidence. She and her friends' case would move up to juvenile court. They'd have to deal with prosecutors. A severe punishment was possible, but the victim didn't want to be involved at all. Kang couldn't do much. He was frustrated.

Who had threatened them? Kang decided to return to the files from the first case. Kang checked the two perpetrators, the sixteen and seventeen-year-old boys. He checked people near them, their family, friends, and social media friends. Kang couldn't find anything suspicious. Both boys had been released due to their age. Kang continued to follow up with them. What juvenile criminals received was long hours of counselling. They seemed to cope well. At least superficially.

Several months after his interview with the orange-haired girl, Kang heard that she had left her school. She had even changed her name. The victim had had a hard time. She had also moved out of the school. Her whole family had left the country. They had wanted a new life. The orange-haired girl didn't want to talk to Kang any more.

More months passed. Kang checked how the orange-haired girl was doing and whether she was involved in suspicious activities after moving. She seemed very quiet. A regular teenage girl, coming and going between school and her grandparents' house. One day, Kang waited for her at the front gate of her new school. When she passed him, he followed her. She was not an orange-haired girl any more. With her black hair in a well-trimmed bob, she ignored him at first. Kang continued to follow her. She walked into a small alley and made sure no one from her school was around. Then she stopped in her tracks and turned back. She demonstrated her unhappiness with her voice.

'Are you still following me?' she asked quaintly.

'No, no . . . you're off the hook. Don't worry.' Kang smiled at her. 'But I need your advice.' She heard him but instead of answering, turned back and walked faster.

'Again, another boy . . . claiming he didn't want to do it.' Following her, Kang continued. She didn't stop, but spat, 'What do you want from me? No one knows who I am here. I live in peace here.'

Kang apologized. 'I don't want to bother you in your new life.' Kang held out a plastic bag. She stared down at it. He pulled her arm gently and put the bag in her hand. She took it. 'Red bean bread. I finally found the bread made with locally grown red bean. It's sweet, but a very nice sweetness.' The girl looked at him. Kang grinned at her. She turned around and kept walking. But she took the bag. Matching her stride, Kang wished that she would smile a little bit.

'I just wanted to check whether you can give us some advice now.'

She was slowing down.

'Several months have passed since that time. Somehow, I keep thinking about you. You are the one who can save more victims. I feel that someone perhaps threatened you to do it. You can tell me now.' Kang said.

She croaked, 'Nothing to say, Detective Kang. I really regret what I did. It won't happen again.'

'I really want to round up this guy. The sooner, the better because the victims are getting younger. This time, the perpetrator is twelve. And the victim is six.'

She stopped walking. But she didn't turn around for a while. She didn't walk back to Kang, but she turned around.

She gazed at Kang and opened her mouth. 'What did he do?' Her voice was sharp. Kang could feel that her heart quaked with fear. Her voice was telling.

'He forced the victim to taste excrement,' Kang answered.

Her eyes flew open. But strangely, she seemed relieved after hearing the crime.

'Leave him alone. Give him some time. Time will pass.' She kept walking then turned around to face Kang once more. She threw one more sentence at him with a muddled face. 'Make sure to tell the boy not to do that any more. Please follow the twelve-year-old boy, not me. He will need some help. He might still have a long and winding road left.'

She walked without turning back again. Kang was still able to hear what she said clearly. 'Thanks for the red bean bread. Your hard work will be ending soon . . . hopefully.'

She walked away fast. Kang lifted his voice. 'Anytime! Call me when you want to have more red bean bread!'

Kang knew that he couldn't push her more. But the age was getting younger. He was sure there was someone behind these cases. Their crimes were different, but it was from the same trap. Now, with her reaction, the orange-haired girl had basically proved that there was another perpetrator behind this. The cases were from all over. They were not related or geographically connected. That meant they were probably virtually connected. But he'd had no luck finding any reliable information. They'd just hired a young technician. That might bring some luck.

Kang was determined to round up the ringleader. The sooner, the better. He walked back towards his car. He felt his feet were lighter. Meeting and checking with her had been a great idea. *But what did she mean? My hard work will be ending soon, she'd said.* He stopped and turned his head back. She was long gone.

Chapter 20
Gun and Jihoon

February 2015

'If you need money, don't worry. I already planned on giving you my money.'

Gun smirked. 'Sure, that sounds great.' Gun and Jihoon were sitting in a room. It was in the middle of the mountains around Seoul. Surrounded by nature, the traditional house was a Michelin star restaurant. You had to take a series of stone stairs to reach this house. You had to make reservations months in advance.

Gun was looking dapper. He had probably thought that it was a celebration for his university graduation. Young and Minsu had probably encouraged Gun to wear a good outfit for this expensive restaurant and expected that Jihoon would tell Gun that he would be his financial godfather for his study abroad.

When Jihoon opened his mouth, Gun thought it was going to be an offer from Jihoon. In a series of text messages, Minsu had reminded Gun to show up at the dinner table. Gun thought of his pathetic father. He'd known for some time that his university tuition fees and allowance were from Jihoon, not from his parents. He didn't care. They gave the money with happy faces. Gun took it with a smile. A happy family.

'Will you stop then?' Jihoon's eyes were desperate.

'Stop what?' Gun picked up a flower-shaped pickle sprinkled with caviar. He put it in his mouth. It was salty. The cucumber should have been colder. His frown demonstrated his displeasure.

'What you are doing is profoundly wrong. You can't do such horrible things to other human beings.'

Either the taste of the cucumber or Jihoon's annoying tone caused Gun to stare at Jihoon with displeased eyes. They had eye contact for a long time, looking at each other in silence.

Jihoon was about to open his mouth but then decided not to say anything. He could see it in Gun's eyes. Gun knew what Jihoon was about to say.

'No, that's my life. You can't tell me what to do and what not to do.' Gun's eyes blazed with fury.

Jihoon felt woozy.

'You owe me. You owe Mini. You should have a happy life. You should be a nice person. You can't throw your life away committing these evil crimes.'

'Are you threatening me? Who the hell is Mini?' Gun gave Jihoon a wolfish smirk.

'She lives in you. You are able to live owing to my girl's heart.'

The secret was out. The one Young and Minsu had not wanted Gun to know. Would the knowledge check Gun's monstrous behaviour? Jihoon didn't know but there was little else he could do. Gun kept silent. He stared at Jihoon with a look of surprise. Suddenly, he understood. With contented eyes and a grin, he said, 'Wow, I thought you were just a tough nut to crack! No wonder you looked so familiar! Now I get it, why my parents gave so much weight to whatever you said. It was not just about money.'

Gun put his steel chopsticks down on the table and clapped his hands. 'You hid yourself so well so far. Just like me. Maybe we really are related!' Gun chuckled.

'You have to live much harder than others, Gun,' said Jihoon. 'You owe your life to Mini.'

Gun thought about his parents' words. Words that he hated, words he despised so much. The girl without a face in his dream was always trying to take Gun's heart from him. That was the nightmare he had every time his parents told him how hard he should live. Gun had thanked the unknown girl when he was small. However, the more he heard from his parents, the more he started hating her. Whenever he did something wrong, Young and Minsu would remind him of how he owed his life to the girl. They never mentioned her name, only said that she was an angel. An angel for their family.

Now, Gun understood why Jihoon lingered around. Why Jihoon smiled at him. Why Gun had hated his smile from the get-go. Gun was forced to feel guilty because he was not nice to this pathetic, wealthy guy in front of him, nor to his parents.

'What a wretched father you are!' Meeting Jihoon's desperate eyes, Gun flashed an off-putting smile. 'So, now you are here, and trying to pull the rug from under my feet. How did you get wind of it? No one was able to find out!' Jihoon's obsessive stalking of Gun must have been the key to his discovery. 'You were my stalker. So, my friend was right. Or you were one of the customers of my business. Or you were stalking me, and you were the patron of my business at the same time.'

Gun had a strong temptation to be more brutal. Jihoon's face seemed to be pleading with him. *Does he see through me? Or does he follow the ghost of his daughter?* Gun guffawed. 'Oh! What a shock! That's why this crazy man stalked me for years and years. You are the father who gave your kid's heart to me. Do I have to show my veneration to you now? No wonder my parents were always acting annoyingly in front of you. But you know what? Your daughter is dead. Her heart is not hers any more. It is mine. And it is my life. I live the way I want to live. And I am a king in this world. You don't know how painstakingly I worked for this game! No one beats me. No one knows how this life makes me feel alive.'

Gun sneered at Jihoon, whose face had become paler. 'Think about it. Why do you think I'm doing this business? Your daughter's heart likes it. Do you know how I know? Whenever I get more slaves and my business becomes more successful, my heart reacts first—beating hard and fast. I do this not because of money. I know you are going to give your money to me. My stupid father cannot hide it. I know just from the look on his face. But you know what? I don't even need your money. I have enough already.'

Gun felt victorious. His heart was beating hard. *Is it beating hard because I'm in front of this guy?* Gun took a long, deep breath and grinned. He picked up the chopsticks again and soaked a piece of raw tuna in *gochujang*. He put it in his mouth. The texture was perfect. Enjoying the cold temperature of the fish, he said slowly with good staccato, 'I do this because my heart loves it. So, you should know that it is actually your daughter who has steered me in this direction.'

Jihoon stood up from his seat. Gun moved his hands forward and whistled. 'Oh, oh. Calm down, man. I'm carrying your girl's heart.' Jihoon grimaced but held back.

'Gun, you act without forethought. Think about it. You have such a bright future. Things will be guaranteed for you.'

Gun got bolder. 'I made myself very clear. I do this on behalf of your daughter.' Gun grinned at Jihoon. Gun's tone was insolent.

'You can't stop me. Or we can expand my business with your money. If you go around with me more, Mini and I can do more fun things together,' Gun said snarkily.

'Sit down, man. Now I feel better.' Gun put his arms behind his body, over the backrest of the chair, exposing his chest, his heart, to Jihoon. 'Now I feel like I know you. You know me. I am taking care of this heart very well.' Gun proudly patted his heart, making a show of how gently he did it with a smile.

'Let's enjoy the food here. So far, it is not that great. I wonder how this place became a Michelin star restaurant. Maybe better dishes will come later.' Gun gnawed at another piece of fish. 'But this is good! You need to eat the cold fish with the gochujang sauce. Making this an appetizer was a brilliant idea!'

Jihoon couldn't move. Jihoon couldn't say anything more to Gun. He felt his mind descend into awful convulsions. Jihoon saw before him a monster who enjoyed cruelty. *He doesn't even have a tinge of guilt. He relishes his game.*

Jihoon tried to calm himself down.

He's deflecting. This is not what he is supposed to do . . . Jihoon felt his throat constrict. Gun was right. He carried Mini's heart. This awful truth was inescapable.

Jihoon recalled Loa—the pain Loa had shown and the curse he had spat out several years before.

I should liberate my daughter from this monster. The sooner, the better. Jihoon's eyes dwelled for a moment on Gun's face and travelled down Gun's chest.

There is only one choice for me.

Chapter 21
Gun with Five Angels

February 2016

It was an odd moment. Two people sitting together. One always trying to catch and the other always trying to release. The former were always evil he should punish. The latter were always customers she should serve. This time, however, was different.

The lucky moon case had already moved up to the prosecutor's office. It was one of the easiest and clearest cases. The criminal had admitted everything. There was incontrovertible evidence. The prosecutor's office didn't know what to do with the victim, though. The clearest case thus opened bigger cases. The more they dug, the more entwined they found themselves in a web. Interpol had stepped in. They were not interested in Jihoon at all. While a large number of agents worked on Gun, there were only two people who were still on Jihoon's case.

Kang and Hana were sitting in Hana's office late one night. The office cleaning lady had also left, making sure that Hana knew there were leftovers in the office refrigerator from their celebration of the merger with another company.

What Hana had heard from her boss was they were going to make a bigger and separate section for clients who were vulnerable due to mental instability. In this crazy modern society, there were bound to be more cases related to mental vulnerability. The boss had bragged they would hire a criminal psychiatrist and some juniors who could help Hana. She had become the representative for this section.

'You would know best.' He had shown a big creepy smile.

★★★

Jihoon had sent a big pay cheque to Hana's firm, requesting her not to take his case, but instead to protect his ex-wife and Gun's parents if they were exposed to the media or misunderstood as accomplices. What a situation. The ex-wife had hired the firm to defend the ex-husband, who had then refused their services, and instead, paid the firm to do something else. An extra request Jihoon had been made—and one that Hana couldn't share with Kang—was that she would represent a teenage girl if Kang or the police found any dirt on her related to this case.

'Kang knows her,' said Jihoon.

Jihoon didn't want to share anything further with Hana. 'If the police try to link her with me, then contact me. You should represent her.'

★★★

Hana saw Kang. He looked tired. *Of course, this workaholic didn't sleep much over the last weeks.* She took out rice cake and orange juice from the office kitchen and put them on her table. Kang even didn't even spare it a glance.

'There is no evidence that he killed others. I investigated each one. Even one clear cut murder would give him a life sentence. You can't even plead extenuating circumstances.'

Kang continued, 'No matter who the victim was . . .'

Hana remained silent. To some people, what Jihoon did was justice. To the legal world, he was a cruel murderer. Hana's suggestion to examine

Jihoon's mental illness was rejected by Jihoon at once. His story could get a lot of sympathy. It could lead to a possible diagnosis of psychotic depression and send him to a well-managed facility.

Kang opened a big envelope on Hana's desk and slid some photos towards Hana.

'What are these?' Hana picked them up. Her eyes narrowed as she looked at each photo.

'All these were taken from Jihoon's house.'

The photos showed a big space. There were six transparent white boards. Each board has a kid's photo and some other photos beneath it.

'It's from the basement. His house is rather big for one person. We scoped his whole place out. Now we know why he needed such a big space.' Hana paused to study one photo. The photo showed one boy's mugshot, below which were photos of him, showing him as he grew.

'This is Ansoo. He received a kidney from Jihoon's daughter.' Hana's eyes widened and she looked up at Kang, who focused his eyes back on the table.

'Jihoon basically stalked the kids who had received his daughter's organs. He had detailed records of each kid. About everything. Ansoo's first girlfriend, his school transcripts. Jihoon had a private agent who followed each kid.'

Hana could not believe what she was hearing.

'Then how about others? Were they all killed?'

Hana could not believe he would do that.

Kang shook his head. He didn't look like he wanted to talk about it.

'Unfortunately, they didn't grow as Jihoon expected . . .'

'What do you mean? What happened to the other kids . . .? I mean the other people?' Hana corrected herself, since they would no longer have been children.

'We already know what happened to Gun.' Hana nodded. Kang picked up each photo and showed each face to her. 'Here is Nomin. He received the liver. The surgery was successful. But his mother took him to Vietnam. They left Korea. His mother was accused of poisoning her mother-in-law. She denied it. But the husband didn't seem to trust his wife. In the end, she was found not guilty. But she still left with her son, leaving her husband. She was bitter and didn't want to return.'

Hana asked, 'Did Jihoon do something to him?' Kang said, 'I don't know. I talked to Nomin. He claimed that he sometimes received strange messages from unknown people, sending long words of moral teaching. He also said he had small accidents sometimes and was beaten by thugs once for no reason. Or, sometimes, he received some money in his bank account. Nomin thought it was from his father. But his father denied it. Nomin's story was not consistent. He said that sometimes he felt someone was watching him.'

Hana stared at the young man in the photo. 'And you found these photos from Jihoon's house.'

Kang nodded. 'Yes, but I don't know how involved he was in Nomin's life. If he was just checking in, or orchestrating everything as Nomin said. Nomin wanted to believe his father was sending someone to check whether he was fine or not, and whether he was growing up well . . . Maybe such belief might not be bad for him.'

Hana sighed, but said determinedly, 'This doesn't prove Jihoon did something to Nomin.' Kang didn't respond. Hana picked up another photo.

Hana went back to the first photo. 'How about him? Ansoo? What happened with him?' Hana pointed at the photo of the boy who had received a kidney from Mini.

'This was perhaps the worst story for Jihoon.'

Hana raised her eyebrows. 'Why?'

'His kidney failed. Or rather, Mini's.'

'Because of the side effects?' Hana gasped.

Kang smiled bitterly. 'That would have been better. Then Jihoon wouldn't have been so bitter about it.'

Hana was having a hard time following what Kang was saying.

'Apparently, that happens. Have you heard of immunosuppression?' Kang raised an eyebrow and asked Hana.

Hana shook her head firmly. It seemed to be a word from a completely new world. 'Immunosuppression?' She repeated what Kang had just said.

'Yes, immunosuppression. When you get a new kidney, the critical condition is that the recipient should take pills to suppress the side effects.' Kang tried to speak slowly so that he could be precise in his explanation of something that he himself had only recently learnt about.

'You mean forever?' Hana asked.

'Yes, forever. Before a kidney transplant, the doctor makes sure that the recipient is willing to take the medicine forever.' Kang shook his head and said, 'I became a semi-expert while I was investigating Jihoon's case.' Kang made sure Hana was following his explanation before moving on to the next part. 'The tricky part is if the recipient is a child, the parents can take care of this and make sure their child takes the medicine. But when they become teenagers, there can be some challenges.'

Hana's eager eyes aimed at Kang showed she wanted to know the next part of the story.

'I don't know . . . it could have been him just forgetting, or maybe it was rebellion. Teenagers don't want their friends to know that they are taking medication. They wouldn't want to even talk about having received an organ . . . Things get complicated when you are a teenager,' Kang added.

Hana unconsciously nodded, thinking about her time as a teenager. It sounded familiar.

'Ansoo seems to be one of those cases. He didn't have any issue after the transplant. He didn't have any side effects. A perfect match. A happy story till that part. His parents were released from giving him medicine and they were sure that Ansoo would be responsible about taking his medicine. But he stopped taking it. He maybe thought he was fine, and his parents were just being pushy without even having enough medical knowledge. Or maybe he just wanted a little control over his own life. He didn't take the medicine for a long time. Of course, that led to side effects to his body.'

'Oh my gosh!' Hana hadn't expected such a story.

'Their efforts over many years went kaput.' Kang snapped his fingers. 'It was gone. The kidney didn't function any more.'

'So, what happened?' Hana's heart pounded. 'Did he die? Did Jihoon get to know about it?'

'No, he didn't die. He was lucky enough to find another donor. I think Jihoon didn't even know about it. Later on, when he came to know, he was angry. Or maybe, he was desperate. Because, in the end, the kidney was from Mini, it was a part of her. Maybe he felt his daughter died again.'

Hana could understand Jihoon, but it was grotesque at the same time.

What would she do if she were in Jihoon's situation?

What about the cornea boy? Hana thought.

Kang must have read Hana's mind. He picked up a photo. The photo showed a slender and pale young man standing. His shoulder was noticeably bent. *Does he have some back issue or is he extremely shy?* wondered Hana.

'This is Loa. Cornea boy. I investigated this case more intensely and talked with his parents. According to his parents, his transplant was successful. He was content in his life and was positive. But his behaviour got out of character suddenly at the tender age of seventeen.'

'Teenage rebellion?' Hana asked.

'No, that would have been better. Ever since he turned seventeen, everything got jumbled up. He started claiming that he was seeing something, some girl. And he knew about Mini. His parents told me that they'd only ever mentioned her name to him once. And it was a long time ago, back when the surgery had been performed. Then, when he was seventeen, he started claiming he knew Mini and that she had come back and she was with him.'

'Was that true?' Hana was shocked.

Kang shook his head. 'No, according to his parents, they were worried that he might have medical side effects or something. They took him to the doctor. And his eyes somehow started having a reaction. It happens and it is not rare in cases of a cornea transplant. Maybe the pressure on his eyes was off. That can lead to hallucinations. In any case, he became paranoid, and he started doing some weird research and talking about spiritual things. His fear created a nightmare. And he then learnt about some weird religion that talked about spirits, curses, and that ruining the body is against God's will. Then this boy refused to get treatment, and started believing what he believes . . .'

Hana read the documents that Kang had shared with her. 'That's why he threw the girl in the Han River.'

'Yes, he said that's what Mini wanted. Each recipient of her body part should make a sacrifice to her. That way she would not be angry.'

'And that's why he did it. But the girl was fortunately saved by people at that time.' Hana raised her face from the document to look at Kang.

'Correct,' said Kang.

'He went crazy when he felt his curse would bring back the horrific itchiness of the past. He had trauma when he was young . . . and he freaked out and took the wrong path and saw truth in the wrong beliefs . . .'

Kang continued, 'That's the moment Jihoon received a phone call from his parents. Loa implanted a crazy idea into Jihoon's head.'

Hana shook her head and said, 'You mean he told Jihoon his daughter wasn't actually dead? Imagine how he felt at that moment.'

'Jihoon started believing he'd actually killed her again. He wanted to make sure. He checked on all these kids to see whether they had symptoms similar to Loa.'

'He frantically tracked down each one . . . and when he saw unhappy stories, he believed cornea boy's crazy idea; that they are somehow cursed.'

Kang caught a look of mixed sadness and sympathy crossing Hana's face and continued. 'I contacted Jihoon's ex-wife. She said Jihoon never contacted her after they separated. With one exception. Well, one exception before the crime. She could hear the waver in his voice over the phone. She said his voice had been leaden, but desperate. He'd asked her repeatedly whether she remembered what the hospital had told them exactly about Mini's death. She had been shocked and had felt hurt. But she said she had also been scared for Jihoon. He had been wailing like a hunted animal that was losing its life. And he had asked whether there was any doubt about Mini's death at that time. But after that, he'd hung up. And there was no contact at all until he called her after the . . . crime. Jihoon told her it was all his fault and said sorry. He told her he had finally found the right person for Mini, but he should be punished because he had acted as God.'

Hana listened to Kang. This part was familiar. She had also heard it from Jihoon's ex-wife.

Kang continued, 'After Jihoon met the cornea boy in prison, he checked Gun. Gun looked to have escaped the curse. He had no trouble in his life, and he had Mini's heart. So, Jihoon seemed to focus on Gun. Maybe he was pleased with how well Gun was doing. He was a top student and was not making trouble. But when he found out about what Gun had been doing, it was his worst nightmare . . . the worst. To Jihoon, Gun was carrying on like the devil.'

'It took time for us to find out.' Kang was rattled and annoyed at the same time. He was supposed to be the one to catch him. The next step was for the police to take the flak.

'It was different though. It is hard to guess what kids at that age are doing. Who would have imagined?'

'Jihoon didn't believe it at first. But the more he investigated, the more the cornea boy's words filled Jihoon's head. And it became a conviction. He thought someone had tried to incriminate Gun. Some big scary gangsters or something like that. So, he wanted to figure it out without telling Gun's parents. He confronted Gun and begged him not to go down that route. Jihoon thought there was no evil behind Gun. But Gun himself was evil. That led Jihoon to the cornea boy's nightmare.'

Hana said, 'That's why he decided to finish the curse.'

'In his ritual way, yes,' Kang firmly replied.

Hana thought about the moment when Jihoon had finally seen the real Gun.

Kang sighed and pushed more files towards Hana. 'I think Jihoon had an especially strong attachment to him.'

'Because . . . he got her heart?' Hana pulled the files towards her.

'Yes, that's why he decided to directly show up in front of him.'

While Hana was listening to Kang, she opened the files.

'After Mini's death, Jihoon went back to his work. Of course, Mini's mother blamed him. It was his devotion to work that had basically killed their daughter. She said that's why she had left him. After her death and the transplants, she said that Jihoon changed more extremely. He became very energetic and started calling those kids *their* kids. And he started working more crazily because he told her he should take care of them. Most parents appreciated Mini's family, but they also didn't want to see them because they felt guilty whenever they saw the couple who had lost their girl and shared her pieces with their children.'

Kang felt thirsty and finally opened the juice bottle. He gulped it down and glanced at Hana briefly. He continued, 'They moved to Singapore, and he jumped into what he was good at—finance and investing in start-up companies. He seemed to work frantically. He earned a lot of money, but his wife left in the beginning. She was scared of the way he talked about those kids. She wanted to have a new life. She said she didn't have a choice. She decamped from him. Maybe she was smart.'

Hana was impressed with how much Kang had managed to investigate in a short time.

'His illusion grew. After his wife left, he only lived for making money. He hired some informants so they could share updates on each kid's life with him.'

Hana raised her eyebrows. 'How did you know that?'

Kang shrugged briefly. 'I met them. They said it was good money. Taking some photos and sending brief reports brought good money. But Jihoon got very frustrated with how each of the recipients had turned out. When they were not as good as he expected, he became furious that they didn't appreciate their lives . . . and everything took a turn for the worse when he met Loa personally in prison.

'So, when the children could not meet his expectations, he became more desperate. And when he heard Loa's words and saw who Gun was, he wanted to take his dead daughter back from them.'

Hana said, reflecting, 'Jihoon thought of Gun as his son.'

'As his daughter, perhaps,' Kang interjected. 'As Mini was living in Gun's body.'

Hana shook her head.

Kang went on, 'That's why, when Jihoon got to know that Gun was doing such horrible things, he tried to change Gun's mind. But it didn't work. Then he got frustrated.'

Hana sighed and replied, 'That's why Jihoon kept saying that he wanted to find a better one for Mini. That's crazy. What kind of love is that? But Jihoon also seemed to suffer a lot. He couldn't believe what Gun was doing. It is ironic that owing to Jihoon we finally found Gun.'

Kang had a frustrated look on his face.

'Then, Gun's case is . . .?' Hana cautiously asked Kang.

Kang said, 'Gun's case just opened. Not as the victim, as the perpetrator. The youngest, but the cruellest and most cunning one. His death is lucky for victims or potential victims. I don't know what to say . . . It would have been good if we'd caught him alive first. Then we might have found out about more crimes through the interrogation. Hopefully, there are no copycat crimes.

'We never thought such a young man would be the ringleader behind all of this . . . He started when he was in high school. We were not looking for someone like him.'

'Who made Gun a monster? He was a normal boy, who studied hard and had a normal family. I wonder how his parents are digesting this story,' Hana wondered.

'Tell me about it.' Kang sighed. 'They were so betrayed by Jihoon and were so angry with him. But at the same time, they were shocked at what Gun had been doing. They had no idea. I can't place myself in their shoes. We can't contact them. They refused to talk with us after we confiscated his computers and notebooks.'

'They don't know what Gun did then.' Hana bit her lip.

'They know, but not entirely . . . the investigation just started. This monster destroyed many people.' Kang thought about the orange-haired girl. They found out that the teacher who had committed suicide after the investigation had been threatened by someone with the ID 'DoGDoG' on the internet. And the person behind that ID was Gun. They must have been related.

'I don't understand. He started committing these crimes when he was in high school?' Hana interrupted Kang's train of thought.

'Yes, or maybe even earlier. He was very good at coding and computer stuff. That's what kids learn nowadays. Early exposure to these modern gadgets. Most crimes nowadays are from the internet. He could have started even earlier.'

Hana gasped. 'But his friends didn't know at all.'

'No . . . no one knew till Jihoon found out.'

'And Jihoon seemed to catch on that we were getting close to him. Now Interpol is everywhere, and we have to cooperate with them and deliver any information we get because Gun also used domains outside of Korea.'

'So, before you could take action, Jihoon did.' Hana now understood.

'Yes. Gun's crimes are huge. It will come out soon in public. There are too many victims.' Kang paused. He was wondering whether there had been any accomplices who had helped Gun. How could Jihoon have found out? Gun looked perfect. His parents, the closest ones, and his friends didn't know anything at all. His internet customers didn't know who was behind it all.

'Gun used his brain for this. He was even ready to escape punishment if he was caught.'

Hana asked, 'Did you find something more?'

'In his computer and notebooks, he had a list of instructions of what to do to receive only a light punishment. He understood the law very well. One of his notes was that it would be beneficial to volunteer somewhere.'

'So, he can get lighter punishment in case . . .' Hana couldn't believe it.

'Yes, that's why he regularly volunteered at the centre for disabled children. Maybe his parents thought he did the volunteer work to gain points for university or maybe they thought he was genuinely a nice boy.'

Is there a pure monster in this world? Hana thought about the 'psycho' from before.

'He even gave online legal advice to people who don't know legal basics,' Kang said.

'Good practice for him.' Hana scowled. She shook her head. 'I don't get it . . . he seems to have a normal family background. He didn't go through any childhood trauma . . . What made him into a monster . . .?'

Kang became reticent.

He finally said, 'There are crimes that we can't explain nowadays. We can't find the reason. He had two completely different faces. No one could match the two to one person.'

Kang thought about Jihoon and the orange-haired girl again.

'No matter what the outcome was, what Jihoon did was horrible. But I will keep taking his calls.' Hana looked sad.

Kang asked, 'Has he changed his mind?'

Hana shook her head slowly. There were two missions Jihoon had given her—the teenage girl and the new owner of the heart. Hana had to keep them from Kang too.

Epilogue
Yeri

28 August 2016

Yeri had hoped to remain a firefighter. Now, she was filling numbers into Excel files. The programme wasn't easy to learn. She had never been good at math.

'Excel does every calculation for you. Your math ability doesn't matter. Just master the programme,' Senior Bang explained kindly.

Yeri smiled at her and said, 'I'm getting there. It is an amazing programme. It looked so complicated at first. But now I feel that as long as I can understand the common functions, I will get used to it faster.'

Senior Bang patted her shoulder and walked away.

Yeri sipped some water. Sitting at her desk from 9 a.m. to 6 p.m. was not easy. She had loved her job. She had been the only female firefighter in the district. She enjoyed tough training. When she had gone through the training, there was little to worry about. She hadn't had to think about herself or her family. Now, in the office, she admired others for being able to sit so long without moving, focused on these boring documents. She sighed.

She patted her cheeks. *Wake up, girl! What indulgent complaining! I survived.*

Her eyes fixed on the picture of the moon, round, and glowing white even in the scrap of a photo taped to the edge of her monitor. She stared at it for a while. The lucky moon had brought her the most luck.

She still remembered that night. Dr Lee had rushed into her room.

'We will go through several tests. If things go well, you will have a new heart.'

Yeri hadn't been able to believe what she had just heard. She had given up by then. She hadn't wanted to continue her life any more. But thanks to the miracle of that night, she'd had a successful surgery.

After several months, she had mostly recovered. She heard that there was some sort of story behind her luck. That was when she had begun wondering who the donor was. No one told her directly. *You have been saved.* Her family was happy. She couldn't remain a firefighter, but that was true regardless of the surgery. She'd also learnt that the fire station would have kept her on in a desk role.

One day, months after returning to the fire station, a woman came to see her. She was about the same age as Yeri. She walked confidently in. The way she looked at Yeri signalled friendliness.

'Hi, Yeri. My name is Hana. May I talk with you?'

Yeri was surprised at the stranger's visit to her workplace.

'Hi, regarding what? It's working hours.' She gave a short smile.

'Oh, sure. I can wait till you are done with work. It's regarding the heart donor.'

Yeri felt like the stranger's eyes were fixed on her heart. It was a surprise. *Donor?*

'You mean, you know about the donor? Are you the family?'

Hana shook her head resolutely.

'No, I'm not. I am . . . a sort of representative.'

★★★

Yeri hurried to the café where Hana had promised to wait for her. She had tried to finish early. But she'd had to finish a budget chart for purchasing equipment. She sometimes appreciated that her work at least gave her a window to know what was happening in the real world of firefighting. She could try to help by finding the latest equipment, or the most reliable. Her work had taken longer than she had expected. Yeri regretted not asking for Hana's phone number. *If she is not there, how can I find her again?*

Fortunately, Hana was waiting for her. Yeri's face was sweaty. Hana checked her watch and understood why.

'Don't worry. I didn't even notice you were late. I was working here. You didn't have to rush.'

Hana flashed a smile and pointed to the pile of papers in front of her. Yeri took a deep breath and smiled. 'I'm sorry. I'm not used to this new position. It's quite slow . . .'

Hana was about to ask whether she wanted to drink coffee or tea. But Yeri's face showed how urgently she wanted to hear what Hana had to say. Hana smiled and collected the papers on the table. Putting them in her bag, she pulled out a yellow envelope.

Hana placed the envelope in front of Yeri and gestured for her to open it.

Yeri saw the envelope and Hana's face behind it. Hana suddenly felt that Yeri could be a good friend. Her innocent eyes caught Hana's attention.

'It's for you.'

'What is this?'

'It's from the donor . . . actually, from the donor's family.'

Yeri cautiously opened the document. She didn't understand what it meant.

'These are his assets. He wants to convey his assets to you.'

Yeri looked up at Hana. This was a surprise.

'Why? I don't understand . . .'

Hana felt that Yeri was nervous. Hana sighed briefly and opened her mouth. Yeri heard the whole story from Hana. She didn't interrupt. She listened. She tried not to miss a word.

Finishing the story, Hana drank her now cold coffee. Yeri stared at the cup for a while.

'So, I have his daughter's heart, and it grew inside a monster.'

Hana looked at her. What she was saying was technically right . . . The small heart from Mini was not only Mini's . . . it had grown and lived with the monster.

'Why is he giving his property to me?' Yeri wondered.

'He doesn't have family left. He is alone on this earth . . . completely alone.'

Yeri stared at Hana and the document. Numbers that looked more like the fire station budget than her income.

Yeri asked, 'What about that mons—I mean, the boy's family? What about them?'

'Jihoon tried to share a part of it with them. They refused.'

'Where are they?'

Hana replied, 'I don't know now. When I tried to contact them last, I didn't succeed. They disappeared.'

Yeri was silent. She watched Hana. Hana looked like a nice person. She felt some sympathy for her. 'A lawyer's work must be tough.'

'It's not easy, especially for me . . . not so suitable for me. This kind of case doesn't help. There is anger and sympathy. It's not easy.' What Jihoon had done was monstrous. He had acted as God. He had thought he could choose who was qualified to live or to die. Hana didn't say anything in front of Yeri. For Jihoon, Yeri was the chosen one. Hana wanted to change the topic.

'How are you? In terms of health? I didn't know anything about organ transplants. But because of this case, I also learnt a bit. I learnt a fair bit about our bodies. These things are complicated. We can be so ignorant and so arrogant. We study hard and we think we know a lot, but we usually understand little about our own bodies.'

'I know . . . I'm on the same page.' Yeri smiled. Hana smiled, too.

Yeri said, 'I'm fine. I'm coping well. Although I can't go on calls any more, I still have a job. Desk duty, as you saw. My family is happy. There are a few people depending on me. '

'Maybe that's why Jihoon chose you . . .'

Yeri looked at Hana.

'It seems that he knows about your background,' said Hana. 'As I know him now, I'm sure that he researched possible recipients carefully and chose you. He must have thought that his money could be used wisely if it was with you.'

Yeri stared at the document. 'It's funny. I was so curious about where this heart is from. I was so grateful. I wanted to know who this person was . . . but nobody seemed to know. Or they didn't want to talk about it. I wondered if it was from a man or a woman? Basically, mine was from both . . .'

Hana said, 'What you said was right though. Mini would be about the same age as you . . . if she were alive.'

'Do you have her photo?'

'No, I don't. Jihoon might have it.'

Yeri held the documents tightly. She put them back in the envelope and pushed it towards Hana.

'I will meet him.'

Hana's eyes widened. *How did Jihoon know this was coming?* He must have researched this girl thoroughly. What Jihoon did was wrong. Whatever sordid history Gun had, Jihoon was not the one who should have chosen who is qualified or not as a recipient. He was not going to be released from prison. He acted as God. His crime wouldn't be forgiven.

Yeri said, 'That is my condition. I will take this after I meet him.'

Hana smiled. 'Jihoon already confirmed that he won't meet you.'

'Then, I won't take it. He can use this money for others . . . he can donate it to others who need an organ transplant.'

Jihoon must have chosen the right girl this time, Hana thought.

'Jihoon doesn't want to see you. That was his big mistake last time, following those kids' lives. He doesn't want to see you. You should understand.'

Yeri was quiet. She took a pen from her bag and started writing on a napkin.

'This is my phone number. You might know it already . . . My condition for taking this money is to visit him regularly.'

Hana tried to push the document back towards Yeri. But she already knew this stubborn girl wouldn't take it.

Yeri smiled. 'I know . . . now my job is dealing with numbers . . . I know what this amount means. It's more than I can make in my lifetime. But that's the condition. Otherwise, I won't accept this offer. I will see him as the father of Mini, who shared her heart with me. That's it.'

Hana looked at Yeri, who continued, now with some hesitation, 'If you don't mind, I would like to ask if you can be there, too, at least one or twice in the beginning. I'm not that good at dealing with strangers.'

'You want me to go with you?' asked Hana with surprise.

'Yes, but not as his lawyer . . . as my company?' Yeri politely asked Hana.

Hana looked at the shy woman in front of her. She couldn't say no. 'Sure . . . but I need to convince Jihoon too. He is as headstrong as you are.' *Why do I see similarities between them?* Hana thought. *He will refuse, but somehow this girl might save him a little from the pain he has been in.* They flashed each other a smile at the same time.

Autumn was coming soon.